To Éoin,

Keep up th...

Cranking up the Motor
&
Other Stories

By

Pat McCarthy

Best Wishes.

Pat Mc Carthy

© **2008 Pat McCarthy**

ISBN: 978-1-905451-84-5

A CIP catalogue for this book is available from the National Library.

This book was published in cooperation with Choice Publishing & Book Services Ltd, Ireland
Tel: 041 9841551 Email: info@choicepublishing.ie
www.choicepublishing.ie

Acknowledgements

To two of my Toastmaster colleagues Jane Duffy and Gerard Gillen. Jane for the story of her love affair with "The Golf." and Gerard for his lovely essay "Morning Glory" on a morning stroll to work. To a very special person Verandah Porche, from Vermont, U.S.A., whom I met in Jamaica, a poet extraordinaire, for her beautiful contribution "Heart to Hearth." To my friend Santiago Trejo from Mexico City, for his love poem, "I would attempt anything." Thanks to Wikipedia, the free encyclopaedia, for information on John Brown, abolitionist.

To my 12 year old grandson Graham Cooney, for his piece "A walk with my dog" who even at his young age seems to have that great gift of observation.

To my wife Mary who said;
"No more procrastinating, go for it."

Thank you,
Pat McCarthy

Table of Contents

Pat McCarthy

I am deeply privileged and honored to contribute to Pat McCarthy's second book "Cranking up the Motor and other short stories." A compilation of poems, and reflective memories, that accompanies Pat on his many adventures and journey's in life.

I first met Pat McCarthy 30 years ago when I was a youth growing up on the Northside of the City, and in particular in the Gurranabraher area. He is a man I respect and admire, and one of the many people who organized and supervised activities for young people. I thank him for his dedication and commitment to young people and the wider community.

This book is a journey of times past; it is humourous, informative, and historical, it gives the reader a glimpse as they say, of, 'The Good old Days.' The Cork saying 'Happy Days' comes to mind as I read some of these short stories. To capture these 'Happy Days' I recommend this book.

Councillor Tony Fitzgerald,
Cork City Council

A Very Special Evening

For James, there would be no overtime this evening. Tonight, St. Valentines' night was, as always, their special night. It was his and Angela's night just like every other Valentines' night had been for the last 7 years. Each evening mealtime was always special, it was a time to sit, relax, and leisurely partake of their meal. Afterwards in the sitting room with a glass of wine, each would relate the ups and downs of the day. Valentines was the most special of all, more special than Christmas, Easter or birthdays. On these occasions they would meet with their close friends or family to celebrate, but Valentines was the one the two of them would always celebrate together.

An accountant with a big clothing manufacturing company James really loved his job. Of course the bonuses it provided with a very good salary meant that they had a very good lifestyle as well. Angela, also an accountant worked more or less freelance. She was able to manage her own business from home. This way she felt she would never be under any great stress, as she would never take on too much work at any one time. And when holiday time came she'd have everything under control.

"Was it luck or was it providence? James preferred to think it was a little bit of each that had first brought them together. St. Valentines' night 9 years ago was when he had met Angela at a mutual friend's birthday party. He fell instantly in love. Cupid had fired his arrow across that crowded room and it had found its mark. Two years later they were married on St. Valentines Day.

Tonight they would once more celebrate that wonderful event. He would purchase the flowers and champagne on the way home, knowing that Angela would have a very special meal ready when he arrived.

2

The silver Candelabra placed in the middle of the table, with four candles waiting to be lit. Also some scented candles would be placed here and there around the dining room. The flowers and champagne would complete the aura of love and romance.

More important than flowers, champagne, or candlelight, was their deep love for each other. Theirs was the epitome of the meaning of a happy marriage. Companionship, trust, togetherness, honesty, and above all, a love that they knew would stand the test of time.

If there was anything missing from their wonderful life together it was children or at least a child. The fact that they didn't have any children had never caused any friction between them, some frustration maybe at times, but never friction. They had been to their doctor and gynaecologist all to no avail. There were some avenues that they still had not explored, but they found these to be repugnant and offending to the person. James thought about all this as he was heading towards home and thanked God that it had not proved to be a major divide between them. Neither had blamed the other for this situation, and both believed, despite all the experts, that the Lord would have the last word on this. He drove up the slight incline of the driveway to the house, pressed the garage remote control, drove the car inside, and with the remote closed the doors again. Picking up the flowers and champagne from the back seat, he went through the connecting door into the kitchen. A couple of pots were steaming on the cooker and the smell of a joint roasting came from the oven. He shouted,

"Honey I'm home."

Angela's voice came from the dining room,

"I'm in here."

James moved from the kitchen to the dining room. It was just as he had pictured it. Angela stood there putting the finishing touches to the table in preparation for their meal. The well laid out table, the

3

candles, two bottles of wine still unopened, one red one white. He placed the champagne on the table and the flowers he handed to Angela.

"I love you" He said "Happy valentines."

Tenderly he placed a kiss on her cheek. She responded with a big loving hug. James went up stairs, showered, changed and returned to the kitchen. It was perfect timing, Angela was at the worktop just about to bring the starter to the dining room table, as she lifted the two dishes he kissed her on the nape of the neck and again whispered,

"I love you."

She turned around, smiled broadly, and said,

"Let's eat."

James opened the red wine and poured two glasses. "Let's have the champagne later on."

As the meal progressed with more or less just small talk about their day, James thought there was something different about Angela, but he couldn't put his finger on it. She reminded him of a flower in the spring waiting for the warm sunshine, holding back, lingering in expectation for the right moment to burst into bloom.

When the meal was finished they put the used delf in the dishwasher. Everything cleared away James opened the bottle of champagne, poured two glasses and both went into the sitting room and sat on the big couch in front of the television. James lifted his glass towards Angela and said,

"To us, may we be as happy in 50 years time as we are tonight."

James reached for the remote control, but was stopped by Angela who said.

"Not just now dear I have something to tell you."

James sat bolt upright a puzzled look on his face.

Smiling Angela continued,

"James take that dopey look off your face it's not bad news. I went to see the doctor to day and I'm two

4

months pregnant. We're going to have our own baby early September."

James nearly choked on his drink hardly able to comprehend what he had just heard. Looking at her lovingly he said.

"Are you sure? What wonderful news and on today of all days. Valentines had always been special for us, but what could be more special than this Valentines, with news like this."

"Yes, as sure as anyone could be, I knew myself, and Dr. Davis confirmed it this morning."

As they cuddled together on the couch their hopes and dreams for now fulfilled, they would look forward to the future. As they lovingly held each other close, Angela whispered in his ear,

"I love you so much."

"Thank God for this, I can hardly believe it, the doctors have been proved completely wrong. After this we can safely say that,

'Prayer is mightier than the medics.'

We must be one of the luckiest couples in the world, and really safe under the wing of St. Valentine."

Amazing Grace

David Burns lay motionless in his bed. All he had were his thoughts. He knew that his time in this world was limited; he also knew that some of his family were in the room, but he could not communicate. His speech, eyesight, and body movements were long gone. His mind was still strong enough and he had not lost his hearing yet, so he understood to a degree what was happening around him.

He kept going back over his life, which by and large had been a fairly happy one. He was the eldest of seven and had always been looked up to by his siblings. His parents had let him know from an early age, that they had expected him to set high standards for the rest of the family to follow. Although he had never reached great heights in industry or other phases in life, he felt that he had not let them down.

Having been brought up in a very catholic home, David was influenced a lot in every thing he did, by the love and loyalty that had been instilled in him by his parents for his family and church. He firmly believed that the Catholic Church was the one true church, and had always, to the best of his ability, lived by its rules. Now for the first time in his life David burns felt unsure, he began to question. Was there really anything out there? Will there be life after death, or had his life been wasted? Had living within the confines of catholic teaching only blunted the real concept of everyday living?

He had worked most of his life as a supervisor in a large factory where women were 85% of the workforce. David loved his job and was very popular with most of the staff. There were a few who didn't understand him, and could not comprehend his integrity when it came to making a few pounds on the sly. They thought he was a fool, and also felt that the company owed them a bit more than their weekly pay. The profits for the last year had always shown that the company was financially in a very good position. So when ever they could, they would cream off a little for themselves.

Even when times were not so good, when the children were young and the wages were small, he had refused to have any hand, act, or part, in the fiddling of hours, bonuses, or under the counter selling of surplus materials. The extra money would indeed have been very handy but he felt it would not be honest, and he would not jeopardise his immortal soul for anything or anyone.

Then the voice cut in on his thoughts,

"What soul? There is no such thing as a soul. How could anything live inside you without you at least having some inkling, some feeling of its presence? David Burns you have lived a life of pure denial. Not a life of love, but a life of fear. Fear of offending something you were brainwashed into believing, something of which you had no concrete evidence of its existence. From cradle onwards you were taught by people who were so full of superstitions that they couldn't decipher truth from fiction."

It startled him and as weak as he was he could feel the evil in its menacing sound. Though not visible to those in the room his whole being was shaking in fear. His head was bursting and he felt it was being bombarded with hot burning darts. He had never experienced any thing like it before. Then he heard another voice. The soothing voice of a woman broke into his thoughts, and for the moment, dispersed those other horrible thoughts.

"Thou O Lord Wilt open my lips,"
And the response,
"My tongue shall announce thy praise."
"Incline unto my aid O God,"
"Oh Lord make haste to help me."
This was the opening prayer of the rosary. Some of the neighbours had come in and joined his family, to pray

for the safe repose of his soul. These were such good people, honest and down to earth.

And then that evil voice again.

"Soul, what soul?" and a hollow "Ha! Ha! Ha! Ha! Haaaaaaaaaa!"

Ignoring it as best he could his mind again travelled back, this time to the kitchen of his childhood home.

The rosary had always been a powerful and popular prayer in their household. Each evening his mother, irrespective of whether his father was home or not, would gather her brood in front of the statue of the Blessed Virgin and recite the rosary. When the rosary was finished she would storm heaven with her own, and everyone else's petitions as well. She prayed for the holy souls, expectant mothers, intemperate fathers, and sick children, those in the neighbourhood doing exams, or going for job interviews. In fact just like the song goes "Uncle Tom Cobley and all."

She would mention each as she went along, and each request had its own "Hail Mary." So their rosary usually took around thirty minutes to finish. The trimmings as we called them, took as long as the rosary itself. David used to think that the trimmings, which were mostly for people outside their family, were a bit of a cop out for those people. Why he thought didn't they go down on their own knees and pray for themselves? He believed that most people in their vicinity would not be all that busy in the evening time, that they couldn't spend ten minutes on their knees with their families. No they would rather approach his mother, who would be known in their neighbourhood as a very religious woman, and ask that she would say a "Hail Mary" for their very special intention.

"Hail Mary full of grace the lord is with thee, Blessed art thou among women."

The voices murmured, almost inaudibly now.

His mothers' face floated before him. A kindly and saintly woman, with never a harsh word for

8

anyone, not even for his father, who could arrive home some evenings with a few drinks in him. She was the one who carefully shaped David's character and instilled in him a love for home, family, and the Catholic Church. And now in what he knew to be his last hours in this world, doubt had entered his mind. Why?

He could hear his mothers' voice gently chiding him.

"Your love for hurling will be the ruination of you. If you spent more time at your homework and less time at the hurling you'd be better off."

But his love of sport did not interfere with his studies as his leaving certificate grades had shown. There had been a time when he had thought about the priesthood, but circumstances at home soon put that out of his mind. He knew had he but hinted this, even vaguely, to his mother, she would have made sure that whoever went without, he would at least be given the chance. A priest or nun in the family would be what every Irish mother would consider the greatest blessing the Lord could bestow on her family. And from then on the family rosary would have an extra petition.

"Glory be to the Father and to the Son and to the Holy Spirit."

The drone of the voices interrupted his thoughts again, and he lay there with only his thoughts unable to communicate in any way. Then he heard the other voice again.

"It's all been in vain you know. You should have lived while you had the chance, it's too late now. All those women who worked under your supervision and you knew of at least six that would have had a clandestine relationship with you, no strings attached. Ha! Ha! Ha! What an idiot you've turned out to be. You only get one shot at life and you should have made the most of it. No! You left it all there for something that doesn't exist. Something you call your immortal soul. Now you're realising there is no such thing as a soul, no such thing as eternity. When you're gone, you're gone, the show is over. "

Why now at this point did he wonder about eternity? He had gone through life so sure, so full of faith, so full of the belief in God, in Heaven, and that wonderful reunion with the loved ones who had gone before him. He had never doubted before. Why should he now?

Eileen had come into his life when he was twenty and she nineteen and they married three years later. They were blessed with two sons and three daughters, and had gone through thick and thin together for nearly forty years. When she died five years ago after many months of illness, the home had been left with a great vacuum. Someone had gone, whom no matter what, could never be replaced.

"Blessed art thou amongst women, and blessed is the fruit of thy womb."

They were still keeping up the prayers for him. What good were prayers if his soul had nowhere to go? What if he didn't have a soul?

'Oh Lord if you are there please come to my aid. Help me do not leave me alone in my misery.'

The priest had been here earlier and spent some time with him. Fr. John is a man who down through the years he could always relate to. They had been friends for a long time, and when time afforded would meet for lunch the odd day. Even when he had been appointed to foreign lands on missionary work, or to just another parish, they had kept up communication, when he had left, David felt so peaceful and so full of hope and faith. After Fr. John's visit it would have been a grand time to die.

These good people gathered 'round his bedside just now had no inkling of the turmoil he was in. His mind was aflame with doubt. Of all times, why now? He felt completely helpless. The nagging was still there. That voice kept repeating.

"End of line! End of line! There's nothing out there, only darkness, a void so black that torment will engulf you, before you are eventually swept away to oblivion."

Then a loud guffawing sound mocked him again, and reverberated around him as if he was in a tunnel. "Ha! Ha! Ha! Haaaaaaaaaaaaaaaaaaaaaa!"

"No! No, no, not this! I do not believe this is happening. I've lived my life to the best of my ability, and kept true to my church and faith."

He was shouting at the top of his voice and no one could hear him.

"This cannot be my reward for holding steadfast in the face of adversity. Lord if you are out there please come to my aid. Do not leave me floundering in the throes of uncertainty. Let me hear your voice and lead me to your kingdom. I am, and always have been your servant."

The helplessness of his situation almost overwhelmed him, when the sound of other voices penetrated his all but unconscious mind.

"Hail Holy Queen mother of mercy, hail our life our sweetness and our hope. To thee do we cry poor banished children of Eve."

Yes, mercy, and above all things hope, that's what he needed now.

With that beautiful prayer which ended the recitation of the rosary ringing in his now almost unconscious mind, a peace descended on David Burns, and suddenly everything became clear. He could see his mother and Eileen at the foot of the bed holding out their hands and beckoning him to come with them, and they would accompany him over the threshold that separated life on earth from eternal life. At last he now knew with certainty that out there was not a void and sudden ending, but life everlasting for those who had lived by the rules. As his soul gently left his body to the joyous sound of Heavenly Choirs, David Burns with his last breath thanked his maker that when it mattered most, his faith had not let him down.

At Ease

Here he sits inside the drawing room window at peace with himself and hopefully at peace with the world. His days for toiling for a living are over, and now, again hopefully, he will enjoy the fruits of that toil for a few more years. Although he loved his work he has never missed it. When on his day of retirement he closed the office door behind him, he handed the key to the receptionist and didn't look back. This was for him the end of an era, and tomorrow would be the first day of the rest of his life.

His dress would indicate he is one who has worked in a clerical or administrative position. To the trained eye his whole demeanour would indicate this. He would be one who would be, during his working career, used to getting up early each morning, shaving, showering, and dressing in fine clothes, complete with necktie. The necktie he wears at the moment though bright is not gaudy and co-ordinates beautifully with the rest of his outfit. Although finished working seven years ago, he still insists on keeping up a certain standard of dress. Sitting contentedly and browsing through an old family album, he reminds one of someone who has mastered the art of growing old gracefully.

When building the house this great bay window overlooking a large expanse of countryside was one of the main specifications. Everybody else seemed to think it was too large, but at the time he insisted on having it large and bowed. In the fine long summer evenings this was the place where he could sit and gather his thoughts and chill out, the cares of the day forgotten for a little while. From here a vast and diverse panorama of countryside lay out before him, one he never got tired of viewing. In the distance the Knockmealdown mountains, and in between him and the mountains,

13

were some beautiful little groves of mature trees. Some clusters of Beech, Oak, Ash, Eucalyptus, and off to the left of him in a piece of boggy land and climbing up the slope of the mountain, a pine forest. The hedgerows around the fertile fields were just now blooming with whitethorn, blackthorn, and other flowering shrubs. The Fuchsia, and Rhododendron with their greenery not yet in full bloom, all looking magnificent in the afternoon sun. Soon the combine harvester would be coming to cut and harvest the grain crops from those fertile fields. First the barley and a little later the wheat and then the oats. All now swaying gently in the soft breeze, that lovely tune "The wind that shakes the barley," coming to mind.

'Oh how lucky I am' he thought, 'Just sitting here and watching the fruits of others labour coming to life, and getting such satisfaction from the glory of it all. The farmers' handiwork coming to fruition through the Lords blessing of sun and rain.'

Another thing he had insisted on was, there would not be a television in this room. This is where he and Liz could sit and read quietly in the evening, or listen to their favourite music. The television and games for the children were located in another room.

Although his body shows signs of his 75years his mind and brain are very active, and he is very alert to what is happening around him. He obviously needs glasses just for reading, as the sound of the door knob turning has caught his attention. He has to remove the glasses to see more clearly. Judging by that glint in his eye and the slight hint of a smile it should be a pleasant diversion. Could it be a member of his family and a couple of grandchildren come to visit? Could it be an old friend dropping in to have a chat and reminisce for awhile? No! It is his dear wife who has arrived with a pot of tea and some freshly baked scones. This is always a disturbance he truly loves. They may not talk all that much, but, just to sit in each others company and feel a closeness that true love and over half a century of togetherness has brought them, is a time to be savoured.

Getting up form his window seat he moves to the table and Liz pours the tea.

"Oh George!" She says, "We have much to be thankful for."

"Yes Liz we surely have. We have so much in our twilight years, others at our age or indeed older are struggling to cope. Those who, unlike us, lived for the day that was in it. They didn't have our foresight to plan for the future. We are indeed a very lucky couple."

"George here's a letter that came this morning from Leo O'Hagan to say Patsy Brogan has died, he was buried last Wednesday. Another long time friend has gone before his maker the light of Heaven on him today."

"Liz it must be three years now since Patsy wrote to us and told us about having to put his dear wife in a home as she had developed Alzheimer's. He had coped as best he could for two years, but in the end, more for her sake than his own, he had to place her in a home. I think when she died just one year later, he felt so bad, that after their long and happy life together, he had let her down. Well Liz, Patsy looked after her so well while he was able I don't think anyone could say he had let her down. I can see them now together holding hands in the presence of the lord and so happy once more."

"George we had a call from Jim awhile ago, he'll be here with the family around 5.30 or 6.00 o'clock. It will probably be a little chaotic and noisy with those three boys of his around, but sure wouldn't it be a lot worse if they never came to visit. The noise of young folk around this house again is always a welcome diversion for us. Mary and her brood will be here tomorrow to take us to lunch in the "Commons Inn," and after lunch take a trip to the garden centre. So that's something to look forward to."

"You know Liz, if Mary hadn't some garden centre to visit would she ever go outside the door. All the plants she buys you'd think she had about four acres."

Finishing their tea and scones Liz returns with the delf to the kitchen and George goes back to his place near the window. He picks up the daily newspaper and reads for a bit. Actually all he does more or less is, to sconce through it, as it's mostly not good news. At this stage in his life he no longer has much interest in what's happening in the world, but likes the snippets of local gossip. Putting the paper on the floor beside the chair, he removes his glasses, presses the lever on the side of the chair to tilt the back and bring up the leg rests. It's time to have a nap and be ready for the invasion of his three wild grandchildren.

Morning Glory

Close your eyes. The alarm goes off. Each morning it's probably the first sound you hear, breaking the silence of the night. This is the time when your ears and eyes awake. In the interval between waking and rising, the creaking of the doors and wooden floors reminds you of the need to keep silent. You hear the morning paper dropping through the letter box and become aware of the world outside. As yet there is very little traffic, but the swish of rubber on concrete heard from the wheels of the odd car that passes all add to your morning wake up.

Is it fine? Is it raining? Is it cold? Stretching across to open the blinds, you gaze out the window and your first observations of the day are made. Within the first few minutes, thousands of images are forming in your mind about the day ahead. It's morning time; and thank God the sun is shining. It's the best time of the day for reflection, the best time of the day for fuelling your senses.

You become aware of the unique individual sounds. The determined and noisy opening of a bedroom door, the rush across the landing to the bathroom, the return to the bedroom followed by the urgent need to have music break the silence. The patter of small feet, followed by the turbulent climb up from the end of your bed. Then, the gentle nudge and the small voice,

"Push over Dad."

The demand for a story and an early morning filled with tireless fun. I'm a morning person; this is my favourite time of the day. After a long night, this is a new beginning, everything starts again. It's the first day of the rest of my life.

To many, morning brings new hope. When a child is sick at night and the parents have walked the floor for several hours comforting the child. Waiting for daylight to come, the world to wake up, the doctor to arrive, the pharmacy to open; how often have we reassured the child? Saying,

"It'll be fine by the morning."

When a person is missing from a ship gone down at sea, or after a falling over board, and the search called off at dusk, how often have we heard?

"The search will resume at first light"

Even those who at the end of the day are troubled with a very big problem, often find a solution in the light of day.

Morning time often provides an inspiration to many poets and musicians. William Stafford, one of the most recognised American poets of the 20th Century would get up in the dark of night brew a cup of coffee, and stretch out on a sofa awaiting the light of morning to write his poetry. Morning time for him was filled with shadows, colours, sounds. He would sit at his desk and put them all together in beautiful and meaningful stanzas.

For some however, morning time doesn't have the same appeal. It can mean, getting into their car negotiating their way from their driveway to the main road. Like blinkers put on a horse, the build up of adrenaline and frustration is generated right from the start, trying to get to work on time. The stop-go movement of traffic hides the sounds and images of the early morning. Instead of arriving refreshed and ready for work, the energy used in getting there, has depleted them of individual space and thinking time.

It doesn't have to be like that! Morning is meant to be an experience of renewing your senses, helping you relax and prepare for the long day ahead. The solution is to get up early, sweep away the cobwebs from your mind, and get the most out of your day.

In the early morning while walking to work, I often see a host of birds, mostly sparrows and starlings, high on the overhead wires, rustling their feathers, chirping noisily and generally getting ready for the day ahead. A Blackbird and a Thrush, up on a television aerial or chimney pot, adding to the symphony that is my Morning Glory. Across the street on her usual early morning perch is a neighbour's cat. She crouches alert and ready to pounce if any bird should venture to pick a morsel from the road below. I don't have the time to wait and see if she is successful. While listening to the dawn chorus, I must rush past the overhanging trees for fear of being used for target practice. Seconds later my real journey starts with the sound of the bugle in Collins Barracks, as Reveille is heard over all the immediate area and the national flag is raised. Somewhere off in the distance a Rooster picks up the buglers note and answers with a shrill 'Cock-a doodle-do.' Truly morning has broken.

Up here on the hill the streets are still silent, and the crisp morning air helps refresh my spirits. I realise that it won't be long now before traffic begins to build up and as I pass apartments and houses I hear alarm clocks going off. I see lights going on in the 2nd floor windows and hear the cry of small children as they awake from their nightly slumber. I recognise familiar faces of other early morning people. Some even whistling, and happy to be able to enjoy their morning glory. Trying to appreciate all this I must also watch my own progress, and for a moment I wonder,

'Will I be late for work?'

Checking my watch I see I'm O.K for time.

Very soon couples will be leaving their homes with their bundled up child or children rushing to meet their childminder or going to their local crèche. The schools will be opening shortly and children will be making their way to the nearest shop, either to purchase a snack and a drink, or meet their colleagues to walk up Patrick's Hill together and start another day in the class room. None look over enthusiastic about this.

Patrick's Bridge is looming now and I'm well over half-way to work. If I'm lucky I'll meet a fellow Toastmaster or two, and from them I'll get a good morning greeting and best wishes for the day. I also see my eye-doctor, both of us going to the same place, but decline his kind offer of a lift. I walk along Camden Quay, Popes Quay, over Northgate Bridge and along Bachelors Quay. Along with the screeching sea gulls I hear the bells from the local church calling to us and reminding us of our MORNING GLORY, and I thank the Lord for affording me this wonderful start of the day experience.

I enter the MERCY with ten minutes to spare, refreshed, ready, and raring to go.

My Ten commandments

Feel good about yourself
Don't judge your own efforts.
Don't dwell in the past.
Look to the future, but, not too far.
Keep lines of communication open at all times.
Be a good listener.
Never go to sleep with an unresolved argument.
Keep remembering money is not God.
Try and be of some help to others.
Don't shy away from love.

Going up

Opening the lift doors on the ground floor the lift operator smiles as eight people come in, and with a friendly,

"Goooing up! Welcome on board folks," he closes the lift doors. The lift glides smoothly upwards, and then suddenly gives a shudder between the 5th and 6th floors and halts.

A lady's voice, a little panicky, is heard,

"Hey! What's the matter? This lift isn't moving."

"Now don't panic folks, I'm sure it's nothing serious."

Then a man exclaims.

"What do you mean by it's nothing serious and don't panic? We're five floors up, stuck between floors, and all you can say is don't panic and it's nothing serious. How do you know?"

"Well Sir, begging your pardon, what do expect me to say? Abandon Ship, women and children first."

"You may not have noticed sir, but I'm in the same predicament as you. I'll phone maintenance now and I'm sure everything will be sorted out very shortly. It won't take them long to pinpoint the trouble and we'll soon be on our way."

The lady again says, only this time her voice more nervous and high pitched.

"Oh my God what was that noise? Is this lift is slipping?" We're going down.

"No, no, Madam, even as we speak that's maintenance working on the motor, or on whatever needs working on. I'll give them a ring."

A voice from the back of the elevator bleats.

"Do, and while you're at it, be sure and tell them not to panic. You're pretty good at that."

Stifling a profanity, he says, "Please madam patience." The lift operator goes to the phone.

"Hello! Maintenance? This is Billy Butlin, operator of elevator number 2. Myself and eight other people are in this elevator right now and it has stopped between the 5th and 6th floors. I wonder could you check it out please.

Maintenance reply to his query,

"Two men are on their way right now Billy, the emergency buzzer in the control room alerted us. We believe it's just a fuse, it shouldn't take long, and remember Billy don't panic."

"Oh great, nobody's panicking, and thank you. Now, there you are folks they're working on it already. I told you there is no need to panic."

An obviously very pregnant lady then chirps in.

"Oh no! My God my greatest fears are about to come true. This is the scenario dreaded by every expectant mother, and now for me it's about to materialise. I'm going to have my baby in a lift."

Billy haughtily remarks.

"Don't worry lady you won't be the first. In my career as a lift operator I've already delivered four babies."

This really makes her panic, and she exclaims.

"Oh my God! I've got a $300.oo an hour gynaecologist on standby, and what do I end up with, a $10.oo an hour smart assed bell hop. Isn't that somethin'?"

"Now lady there's no need for that kind of talk, and, I am not a bell hop. I'm only trying to take the stress out of the situation."

"I'm only trying! I'm only trying! You've made the phone call, now shut up, and don't give me any more of that bell hop come midwife stuff either."

A man produces a little container of peanuts and shares them around. The very pregnant lady refuses, and admonishes the gentleman.

"Peanuts! Is that all you can come up with, are you trying to destroy the health of everyone in this lift by increasing their cholesterol to an all time high? Do

23

you not realise that for every peanut one eats you've got to run up and down the stairs thirteen times, just to get rid of the goddamn thing. Peanuts ha!"

"Don't worry about us lady we'll look after our own butts. And looking at you and our situation at the moment, I think we'd all be much better off if we had taken the stairs."

Then the other lady her voice a little shaky says,

"He's right you know, you're not the only one in this lift who's got something wrong with them and is going to see their specialist. If this lift has blown a fuse it will be repaired quickly, but lady if I blow a fuse you may not be so lucky. So give us a break madam and button your lip please."

"Oops! What was that?"

"Please don't panic everything is under control. These men know what they're doing. They're professionals."

Then this other lady pipes up.

"They're professionals! That's no guarantee they know what they're doing. Last week I had a plumber in and he nearly sank the whole goddamn house before he fitted the right washer, or, whatever he had to fit."

From the back of the elevator a voice chimes in.

"She's right you know sometimes a handy man is better. Some professionals are just a bunch of know-alls."

The pregnant lady butts in again.

"I'm sure they know a lot more than our know-all bell hop here, who despite his wonderful knowledge and outside calmness, is at this moment I'd bet, ready to crap in his pants."

"Lady I must say this again, I am not a bell hop, and any more of that kind of talk and you will be barred from travelling in this lift for the future."

"Ha! Ha! Ha! I ask you, now isn't that somethin'? He's going to bar me from his lift for the future. Does it look to you people that we have a future? At the moment it looks as if we might just become part of this goddamn thing very soon."

The peanut guy retorts.

"Look you miserable old cow just shut your gob, if you're feeling like that why don't you kneel down and say your prayers. And while you're at it say one for all of us."

But not to be outdone, she has the answer.

"Oh a pious gentleman and a preacher into the bargain. He's already got everybody's cholesterol sky high and now he wants to raise our souls as well. My! My! What next I wonder?

An appeasing gentleman's voice butts in.

"Look ma'am I have been stuck in a lift before and the best way to ride this incident out is, to stand quietly and talk as if we're old friends. Not just acquaintances brought together by some mechanical malfunction of an elevator. You'll see everything will work out O.K."

The phone rings. Billy picks it up.

"O.K. Thank you very much guys. Well ladies and gentlemen we're on our way"

Checking his watch he tells them.

"I know it was like an eternity but it was just eight minutes. All's well that ends well. Anyone for floor no. six?"

The pregnant lady says.

"Yes I am."

The door opens and Billy trying to have the last word says.

"'Bye now lady and good luck, guess this is my lucky day, I don't have to don my mask, hat, white coat, or rubber gloves, and thank goodness my lift is not going to resemble a labour ward."

But for him no such luck. As the pregnant lady is just going out the lift door, she turns on her heel, looks him straight in the eye, and says.

"Oh yeah! I don't think at any rate, my baby could have survived much longer, with the smell from your bad breath, your B.O., and your awful silent farting, I don't think anyone of us would have lasted much longer in there. Have a nice day."

And leaves behind a very red faced lift operator and seven smiling faces.

Big News

Jimmy O'Hara was walking down the narrow country road to the village of Shady Grove Post Office to draw his pension. He was enjoying the stroll on this beautiful spring morning. The birds such as the Thrush, Blackbird, Lark, were all in fine fettle adding their musical note to this delightful morning. Even the cawing of the crows in Molloys rookery sounded great this morning, and My God the fresh air, one could not put a price on the fresh and clear air. As he came abreast of Harry Hickeys cottage he saw Harry leaning on his gate and seeing Jimmy, Harry exclaimed,

"Hey Jimmy is it true?"

"Is what true Harry?"

"You mean you haven't heard about the UFO?"

"Heard what Harry?"

"My God Jimmy, you must be the only one in the parish that hasn't heard about it."

"Harry what are you talking about, is it some disaster or other?"

"Worse Jimmy boy worse, disaster is too small a word for it. It will be a lot more than disastrous if someone doesn't do something about it quickly."

"Please Harry slow down, and tell me what's about to happen."

"I don't believe it; you stand there and tell me you haven't heard about Paddy Morgan and his encounter with a space ship last night."

"Space ship indeed, Ha! Ha! O.K. I haven't heard about Paddy Morgan. Has he been in an accident, or has he been thrown into jail. Is he in some kind of serious trouble, or as you say have little green Aliens spirited him away?"

"Jimmy you're acting as if you're on another planet."

"I'm not Harry, I just can't make head nor tail about what has happened to Paddy Morgan. Has he been murdered or something? Just get to the point"

"No he hasn't been murdered. I'll tell you what happened to him, Oh poor Paddy It's taken a hell of a lot out of him, but, I still can't believe you haven't heard."

"I haven't heard Harry, so will you please tell me. After all he's always been a very good friend and neighbour?"

"My God the poor fellow must have got an awful fright. When I met him at his cottage gate a while ago he was really shook up, he was the colour of chalk and this happened to him last night."

"Harry you still haven't told me, come on stop beating around the bush, out with it."

"Amin't I telling you, but it's not an easy thing to relate. Paddy says Councillor Hannigan will probably have to go to Dublin to try and drum up some support from the Army. He doesn't think our F.C.A. men would have the fire power or the know how, to handle the situation as it looks now. He's expecting the councillor to arrive to talk to him very shortly."

"Harry what the hell are you talking about? It can't be all that serious that we have to muster up the troops."

"Ah Jimmy! It's easy for you to talk to be so flippant about it, when you don't understand the seriousness of the situation. And maybe before this day is out our village of Shady Grove may be annihilated. Now how do you feel about that?"

"Harry you're obviously not going to tell me, so I'll mosey on down to the village and find out what the trouble is. According to you our village hasn't all that much time left."

"My God Jimmy but you'd try the patience of job, aren't I telling you all about Paddy Morgan and his terrible experience on his way home from Bontys pub last night. I know he had a few in him, but that's not to take anything away from what he saw and heard with his own two eyes and ears."

"O.K, Harry one last time, what happened?"

"Well it seems Paddy Morgan was walking home all on his own last night when he heard the sound of shots. Then this very bright light lit up the whole of one of O'Neill's fields. That big 10 acre one just beyond the Pound Cross. O'Neill had planted that field with corn a month or so ago, and it was coming on nicely. The light held for a couple of seconds, then, there was a fierce explosion and the light went out. As the light went out a cylindrical object shot from the middle of the field up into the night sky, belching flame as it went, never to be seen again. It was a good job that he didn't have too much to drink, as he never stopped running until he reached home. Rumour has it that it was a space ship and having landed to find its bearings, shot away out to space again. So now Jimmy what do you think of that?"

"A space ship how are you! Have you any idea what the size of a space ship is? Even O'Neill's 10 acre field wouldn't be big enough for one to land in. You know Harry exaggeration should be your middle name, space ship indeed."

"O.K. Jimmy, Mr. Braveheart if you feel all that courageous, why don't you go and see for yourself."

"That's just what I'm going to do right now, and Harry, why don't you come with me?"

"I don't know Jimmy; the security is probably very tight up there. I'd say we wouldn't be let within a mile of the place."

"Harry from where we are at the moment it's not even a ¼ of a mile to O'Neill's field."

"O.K. Jimmy but if there's anything fishy going on out there I'm out of it like a rocket, and I mean, a space rocket."

So the two friends walk in the direction of O'Neills and no sign of Army, F.C.A., Airforce, or even a Gárda. As they pass the field before the one in question Jimmy spots a half yellowy object in the gully near the side of the road, checks it out and sees that it is about three feet long, round and fairly scorched looking as well. Just as if someone had pulled it out of a fire. Turning to Harry he says,

"Ah! Probably something thrown from a passing car or van, some people have no respect for the countryside."

Thinking no more about it or how it came to be there, both headed for O'Neill's 10 acre field. When they arrive at the field, there's Bill O'Neill scratching his head in bewilderment, and looking at this crater in the middle of the field. Two of his sons were also looking very bewildered, as they walked around the periphery of the field.

Jimmy and Harry entered the field and Jimmy asked Bill O Neill.

"Hello Bill, beautiful morning Thank God. Bill what's the matter are you missing something?"

"Good morning Jimmy, Harry, yes as it happens I am missing something. Last night I set a gas bottle with an attachment that would let off a shot every four minutes just where this crater now is. It was to scare the birds or rabbits away from the corn, and give it a chance to grow. Not hearing any shots this morning I decided to check it out and this is what I find. I met Paddy Morgan on the way up here and he starting talking a lot of gibberish about blinding lights, shots, explosions, and space ships, when he was on his way home from Bontys last night."

Taking the situation in as he saw it, and knowing a bit about some of his neighbours and what they might be up to at night, Jimmy exclaimed,

"Hold it! I think we're talking about a funny coincidence here. For a start your gas bottle with no bottom in it is in the ditch just down the road. It strikes me that the young Sullivans from the cottage yonder were out dazzling rabbits last night and just as they lit up this field your gas bottle exploded. Now Paddy Morgan who happened to be on his way home at that time with a few pints in him, misinterpreted the whole situation and panicked. Unfortunately Harry here met Paddy a while ago got the whole screwed up story from him."

"Well what do you know?" Exclaimed Bill. "You could be right. I guess that gas bottle done more damaged to the field and corn than all the birds and rabbits in the parish. But! Thank God no one was hurt."

Calling to his two sons to join them Bill explained to them what in all probability had happened. The five surveyed the crater for a short while more, and lifting his cap and scratching his head again, Bill said,

"Well there's not much more we can do here now, let's all go down to Bontys and have one on me."

Passing Paddy Morgan's cottage on the way they gave him a shout. When he heard about the Sullivans, the dazzling, and the gas bottle, they all had a good laugh. It took Paddy a bit longer than the others to see the funny side of the incident, as he feared he would be slagged for along time to come about space ships and little green men. But then he shrugged his shoulders and thought, 'So what?' and was more than happy to join them at Bontys.

Michaels school picnic

While on a visit to my sister and her family in Silver Spring, Maryland, U.S.A. in April 1990 myself and my wife Mary, were invited to our nephew Michael's school picnic. It was a glorious day, the sun shone brilliantly with just a hint of a breeze. It was such a pleasant day that most were in light summer wear, and most of the kids in their pelt, all were in a party mood and enjoying this very fun day. Some came with buckets of chicken, coolers of soft drinks, and lots of other goodies. Others came, set up their barbecue, and started roasting chicken wings, sausages, spare ribs, and steaks, and all sharing with each other. The men folk dressed in their best bib and tucker were in charge of the barbecuing. There was an overall funfair atmosphere of jolliness and camaraderie. One of the best things for the children was the free pop corn stand, and the bouncing castle, most of the time filled with happy screaming children bopping up and down to their hearts content.

Teachers, parents, pupils, brothers, sisters, grandparents, aunts, uncles, and even some neighbours and friends, all joined together to make this an unforgettable day. It seemed even those who would not normally pass the time of day with one another forgot their petty grievances, real or imaginary, to join together on this day. There was just one prohibition, "No Alcohol Please." This rule was strictly adhered to. I didn't see one of this crowd of around 400 people break this rule.

Of course there were the usual raffles to help to defray school expenses, with all prizes sponsored. However, there was one event where one bought a balloon for $1.oo, we bought two each; these would be released into the atmosphere later in the day.

Indeed what a happy family orientated day it turned out to be and the school had a few more dollars added to its coffers. When the party was about to end we went to the gas point and had our balloons blown up. When we had done this we then attached a label on each with our nephews name and class number on it and asking who ever found the balloon to return the label to the school. There was a prize for the pupil whose balloon went the farthest. We all then assembled in the middle of the school playground. At this point, even though some were really tired, the excitement of the kids had to be seen to be believed. Each hoping their balloon would be the one to travel the farthest.

The Principal then started the count down, 3, 2, 1, go! With one mighty cheer the balloons were set adrift. What a sight! Hundreds of colourful balloons floating lazily skyward and then dispersing in different directions. We all kept looking until the last one had gone out of sight. There was a lot of speculation on how far a balloon would travel, and distance estimates varied greatly from a 1/2 mile to 50 miles. Someone even ventured 1,000 miles, and was laughed out of the field, as it was explained to them that atmospheric conditions and other things would have a bearing on the distance the balloons would eventually travel. There was just one thing though that nobody only I thought of. Making sure that no one had seen me, I cautiously removed the label from one of my balloons before letting the other one off. I then punctured the one I kept, and unseen put the label and the remnants into my pocket.

Having two more weeks still to go on our vacation, I decided that, I would keep the label and punctured balloon until we got back home to Ireland. From Ireland I would send the label and the punctured balloon back to the school, and our nephew could claim that his balloon must surely have gone furthest distance, having travelled 3,000 miles across the Atlantic. A couple of days after we arrived home I wrote to the principal of the school. I told him how I was walking around my garden when I picked up this object which resembled a remnant of a balloon with this note attached. From what I could make out it was released from somewhere in the United States a couple of weeks earlier, it must have been propelled by the Trade Winds across the Atlantic, and landed in my garden in Cork, Ireland.

Amazed, the principal after reading this letter, called a meeting of all the teachers and board of management for the following Friday evening to discuss this phenomenon.

I've been told since, that the principal got somewhat elated, as he could hardly believe his eyes when he read the letter. An ordinary latex balloon to travel 3,000 miles across the Atlantic. Surely this must be a record and should be reported to the Aeronautic Authorities, at Cape Canaveral, it should get national if not international recognition. The remnants and label would have to be sent to a laboratory for tests, and then would probably end up on permanent exhibition in the Smithsonian Institute, in Washington D.C. Their school would be front page news for at least a week. T.V crews complete with satellite dishes would be arriving to interview himself and the pupil whose name was on the card. This would probably be the main topic on Fox News for sometime.

At the time there was a lot of fuss as teachers and pupils tried to comprehend the incident and what it could eventually mean to the school. The news spread like wildfire about Michael's balloon and its unprecedented journey across the Atlantic to Ireland, it seemed unbelievable. While a lot of the talk in the school was all about the balloon and that the prize for the event had already been presented. The name of the winner had been posted on the school notice board, and also, complete with photograph, in the school bi-weekly magazine. The prize had been sponsored by one of the downtown sports shops. It was a $300.oo sports gear voucher, had already been given out, and more than likely been used by the pupil who had won.

At the meeting on the Friday evening everyone was in a quandary as to what was best to do. The ideas and solutions came fast and furious. There was also an atmosphere of excitement in the room. Some wondered if an astronaut or two would come and visit and give their theory on this aeronautical happening.

Then one of the teachers, who was biding his time to have his say, took the wind out of their sails. He remembered that two people from Ireland, an aunt and uncle of one of the students were on holiday in Silver Spring at that time and had attended the picnic. This must surely account for the balloon's journey of 3,000 miles east. So the conclusion was soon reached, it was Aer Lingus and not the trade winds that had propelled it on its journey.

When they realised that this was indeed more than likely the case, spirits were, to say the least, a little deflated. When they also realised that they had been hoodwinked by a cute Irish man, all had a good laugh. An account of the incident was printed in the next issue of the school magazine. A copy of the magazine with the account of the incident was posted on to us. So we had a good laugh too.

The Golf

It was 1997 when the relationship started, coincidently the month was November. I arrived home with my new acquaintance, and waited anxiously for the comments of my family and friends. To my delight everyone approved of my choice. My new Volkswagen Golf had passed the test.

It was purchased like many a car at that time, under the Governments innovative;

"Get you to spend your money faster scheme."
I.e. the old scrappage scheme. So with the €3,000 from the scrappage scheme I had the deposit and I was now the proud and first owner, of a brand new shiny priestly black Volkswagen Golf car.

As it was my first time to purchase an in-date car I vowed I would treat it with the highest regard. Now, that I had joined the "New car brigade" I was determined to update every year and stay in this league. There and then I made a bargain with my new acquaintance, already more than an acquaintance actually. It was love at first sight.

Firstly, I would take it to the main dealership for its service and not to the local garage. In that way it would acquire the best reference stamped in its book for future sale.

Secondly, I would drive the longer route to my destination rather than taking the shorter potholed one, thereby eliminating any possible chance of obtaining irritating rattles, and keeping the tyres intact.

Thirdly, when the ditches up to the house became overgrown with briars I promised to cut them personally. In this way the car would keep its good looks.

There would be no muddy boots worn in this car, no food or drink consumed, and definitely no late night bags of chips. In return my car would keep its value. In a years time I would be able to trade it in for another new shiny model, thereby remaining in "The new car brigade." The cost would be minimal, and I'm sure you'd agree a very fair and simple bargain.

Almost immediately the car began to repay me for my consideration and respect. I became actively engaged in conversations with my male work colleagues, on such issues as engine capacity, fuel consumption, abs brakes, power steering etc. Apparently the Golf Gti was a car that many men had aspired to in their early driving years. Indeed some of my male work colleague's first car had been a Volkswagen Golf.

It didn't seem to matter that mine was the basic model and not the jazzed up sports one. It had the label and that was all that mattered. I was bonding with my male work colleagues like never before. I learned a lot about cars that winter but mostly I learned a lot about the male mind. Unfortunately circumstances didn't allow for the changing to a newer model after the first year. I didn't mind too much, it was still my pride and joy.

With out realising it a strong bond in our relationship was developing. I wasn't so conscious anymore about the wearing of muddy boots or the consumption of the odd bag of chips late at night. When I noticed a few blemishes on the body, I didn't panic. When I lost yet another wheel trim in a pothole I didn't spend hours searching the ditches for it.

While neither of us was actually keeping to our side of the bargain, we were slowly but surely growing very familiar with each other. In our case familiarity did not breed contempt, it bred content. By the end of the second year I had a rethink on my life style choice, of being a member of the "New Car Brigade," and I decided this was no longer for me. Making this choice our relationship progressed even further. I now took the car to the local garage for its service, and I didn't feel guilty about paying the cheaper rate.

The car, like many a relationship, ran smoothly for the first couple of years. Then of course just as the guarantee period was up a technical problem surfaced. The indicator ceased to indicate. Probably some slight inexpensive repair to a switch or wire would sort it out. Or, so I thought. Then it was explained to me that the indicator light was broken, and as all car lights were connected in one control box, this box would have to be replaced. That replacement turned out to be a little more expensive than what I had anticipated. But, I put it down to teething troubles.

Shortly after that incident I also found out that that the wheel replacement for the Golf was a lot more expensive than I had expected. No matter how hard one tries to avoid potholes, it's almost impossible to avoid the newly formed ones. By the time I had paid for the annual service, I wasn't ready financially to part with the Golf. To cover my disappointment, I thought to myself as in the Johnny Logan song, "What's another year?

It was so reliable, had never let me down, and at this time I felt the need to personify the car. I started to refer to it as "She." It was now 2002 and before I knew it we had arrived at another milestone in her life, the N.C.T. I remember well driving her to the N.C.T. centre in Macroom, and on that day I also remember asking myself the question, "If she passes will I trade her in?"

How would I feel without her? After all she had been a part of my life for the last 6 years. I had taken her for a check up the week before the test, so that everything would be in order for the examination, and it was. She passed with flying colours.

When the examiner handed me the N.C.T. certificate and said, "You have her in great shape, she's a credit to you."

Her fate was sealed. We were a couple, a team. Recognised and envied by friends and neighbours alike. As we drove around wherever, the bond between us was so strong, and I felt so proud, that there was no way I could trade her in now.

So, now to the present. She has just passed her second N.C.T. and you will definitely not be reading in the "Evening Echo" free ads,

"1997 Volkswagen Golf for sale, one previous owner."

Heart to Hearth

Old fangled snow is the stuff of yarns:
The saga of our sagging barns;

The sled run down to kingdom come;
The ox roast when the twins got home;

Those purple finches on the branch
Whose wings could launch an avalanche.

Myths are throws crocheted near stoves
As the town truck garlands icy roads.

Verandah Porche
Winter Solstice, 2007.

Peace

The olive branch and snow white dove,
Be our symbol shining bright,
Don't curse the deeds of bitter men,
But show the way and do what's right.

So gather 'round and be as one,
Join our hands and never cease,
To do our bit for all mankind,
And pray for everlasting peace.

Love thy neighbour as thy self,
These are the words of Jesus,
So why not hold them in your heart,
And put them into practise.

Harpers Ferry

Travelling the highways of America in the back seat of a Chevy, one wonder's where all these cars, campers, articulated trucks, inter - state buses, and other vehicles are coming from, or where they are heading for.

It seems that at any given time most of the population of the U.S. is travelling as one, the length and breadth of the country. It doesn't matter if you're on a dual carriageway or a five lane highway, every lane is full. All are moving in unison in the same direction. It's like a non - stop production line. Of course all that is needed is one kink in the conveyor belt, one lane hopping idiot, and all hell breaks loose.

The constant whine of rubber contacting speedily with tarmac or concrete gives you a relaxing feeling, as countryside and signposts zipp by. Dozing sleepily in the back seat, not really heeding your surroundings, you are suddenly brought back to the present by the sudden unexpected quietness. Then you realise you have left Interstate 340 and heading down a narrow country road. You catch sight of a sign that says,

"Harpers Ferry Two Miles"

This road looks magnificently beautiful in its early summer garb, with beautiful blossoming hedgerows. In these hedgerows there are several shrubs and trees, such as Eastern Redbud, Cherry Blossom, Wild Crabapple, and many more. There is a medley of colour, and pleasant aromas.

Shortly you pass another sign that says,

"Welcome to Harpers Ferry, Cradle of American Freedom."

The road dips sharply into a valley between old world houses and shops with names like "Country Junction," "Elegant Junction," "Grape Expectations,"

42

"Herb Lady," and a B&B called "Sweet Dreams and Toast." This last one beckons to you with an enticement to over night here, and maybe you will.

When you reach the little hamlet like town one thing that hits you immediately, apart from its setting, is the lack of motor vehicles on the street. Just one police car and a sign that says,

"No Parking, proceed to Parking Area."

When we stop to ask about this, one policeman leaves the car, and points in the direction of the parking area. He also explains that parking is not allowed in the town or the town's vicinity. This parking area is two miles outside of town. When you get to the parking area there is a $5.00 fee, which entitles you to a return trip on the bus in to town and back. Harper's Ferry has found its way into the 20th century, with the lure of the tourist dollar very much on its mind. As the bus weaves its way down this narrow wooded road, you hear the sound of the Shenandoah River as it flows soothingly on your the right down towards the town. One is saturated in peace and the stopping, if only for a very short while, of time. The trip to town is well worth the $5.00. In the town there are quite a few walking around taking in its beauty, and thinking no doubt, how this small place had such a huge impact on American history.

Harpers Ferry is situated on the left bank of the Shenandoah River, and the right bank of the Potomac. The town nestles itself comfortably into the giant V created by both rivers, as they carry on as one to empty themselves into Chesapeake Bay. Standing on a rise overlooking the town it's hard to fathom that this beautiful hamlet was, on a number of occasions devastated by the flooding of these two great rivers. The high water mark from these floods can still be seen around twenty feet, or higher, up the side of the highest houses in the town. Some must have been covered completely.

For all its beauty and present day calmness Harper's Ferry was once the scene of bloodshed and violent confrontation, and has gone down in history as the place where the first shot was fired in the fight for the abolition of slavery.

On a damp chilly night the local G.P., of this small town Dr. John Torrey was awakened by gunshot followed by a scream of terror. He got out of bed and looking in the direction of the railway station he thought that there was more than the usual hustle and bustle coming from there at such a late hour. He dressed and went to see if his services were needed. They were. Hayward Shepherd a free Negro and porter at the station had been fatally wounded. He had failed to halt when a gang of armed men headed by one known locally as Isaac Smith had challenged him to do so. The free Negro must not have realised the seriousness of his situation, or may not have understood the command given and advanced too far out from the station. However at this stage he had lost so much blood, that there was nothing Dr. Torrey could do to save his life.

Hayward Shepherd was in effect the first man to be killed when John Brown and his followers struck their blow against slavery, which still besmirched Dixie in 1859. Smith and his men had seized the armoury, which was adjacent to the station. Their purpose being to liberate the slaves in the area of Harpers Ferry.

Born in Torrington, Connecticut, John Brown took on the cause of the American Negro slaves. He made it his life's work to abolish slavery in all its forms. He was a tall thin man, dressed in rough homespun shirt, and heavy military type pants, long greycoat, riding boots, wide brimmed floppy hat, and most of the time unshaven. He was not a pleasant sight, and even though he looked every inch a renegade, he had great compassion for the plight of the American Negro. His heart was with the slaves who had suffered terribly at the hands of the big land owners. From an early age his father had shown great hostility to slavery, and instilled in young John Brown a hatred of slavery that would follow him for the rest of his life.

In 1834 in Pennsylvania he started a project among sympathetic abolitionists to educate young Negro's. He dedicated the next 20 years of his life to this and similar ventures; this entailed many sacrifices for him and his family. John Brown and his five sons travelled to Kansas territory which was then the center of the struggle between pro and anti slavery forces. Under John Browns' leadership his sons became active participants in the fight. Many acts of murder were committed against the pro slavery adherents, and his success in withstanding a large party of attacking Missourians at Osawatomie in August 1856 made him nationally famous as the foremost defender of civil rights for blacks.

Aided by increased financial support from abolitionists in the northern states in 1857, John Brown began to formulate a plan that he had long entertained, to free slaves by armed force. He secretly recruited a small band of supporters for this project, and in the Blue Ridge Mountains of Virginia he set up a refuge for freed slaves. After a number of setbacks, he finally launched the venture in October 1859 with a force of 18 men including his five sons.

Not able to do much for the porter, the doctor saddled his horse and rode to the seat of local government in nearby Charlestown. After arriving at the military barracks here, he explained the situation as he saw it back at Harpers Ferry. The O.C then called out the local Militia and headed for Harpers Ferry.

John Brown, whose experience up to this consisted mainly of leading a bunch of guerilla abolitionists, whose aim was to free every Negro slave south of the Maison-Dixon Line. His group seized the Arsenal at Harper's Ferry, West Virginia, and took control of the town. His success was short lived, for instead of taking up an offensive position he occupied a defensive one within the arsenal. Here he was surrounded by the militia from Charlestown, which was reinforced on October 17th by a company of U.S. Marines under the command of Robert E. Lee. Ten of Browns' men including two of his sons were killed in the ensuing battle, and he was forced to surrender.

Brown thought that when word of his stand at Harper's Ferry became known, all the slaves in the immediate area would rally with their support, and victory would be theirs. In his eyes the unthinkable happened, many of these slaves didn't want to be freed. They had been born into slavery and this was the only environment they knew. They feared contact with anyone or anything outside the plantation. They were happy in their ignorance of what the outside world had to offer, and probably for most, freedom was something they wouldn't be able to cope with.

John Brown was arrested and charged with treason and murder. He distinguished himself during his trial by his eloquent defense of his efforts on behalf of the slaves. Convicted, he was hanged on December 2nd 1859 at Charlestown, Virginia. For many years after his death John Brown was regarded among abolitionists as a martyr to the cause of human freedom.

John Brown is remembered mostly for his efforts, by the song dedicated to his compassion and Christian spirit,

"John Browns body lies a mouldering in the grave,

But his truth is marching on."

After a nice evening meal in one of the local restaurants we decided to take up the invitation of the B&B "Sweet Dreams and Toast" and stay the night. Later in the evening before settling down for the night, we had the pleasure of once more strolling leisurely around this "Cradle of American history." Tomorrow we would travel back at our ease, to Silver Spring, Maryland.

Personally for me Harpers Ferry was the most rewarding experience of my trip to the U. S.

St. Patrick Missouri

Unlike the Holocaust, which some deny vehemently ever happened, no one has declared as untrue that terrible national calamity that hit our shores during the Great Potato Famines of 1845 to 1851. This was a time when the population of Ireland was reduced by almost 2 million to just over 6 million. At that period in time two thirds of the people depended solely on agriculture, and almost entirely on the potato as their staple diet.

To try and stave off to some extent the suffering, and indeed the complete annihilation of the Irish peasant, soup kitchens were opened up in many parts of the country. These soup kitchens would provide each member of the family with a bowl soup and a little square of hairy bacon in the bottom of the bowl, and for the most part were started up by Protestant zealots who demanded that a religious form be signed before any soup was served and that those who would benefit from their philanthropic deed would leave behind Catholicism and become Protestants. Many signed this form and from that time forward were branded with the humiliating name "Soupers." A little verse at the time went like this;

"They sold their souls for halfpenny bowl,
Of soup and hairy bacon."

Personally I believe that this was very unfair to stamp those families with this awful name which would stick to them for generations to come. If you had five or six young children, had been evicted from your little holding, and if you didn't sign this document, you would have to watch your family die of starvation in some cold and damp ditch. When eventually things got better, most turned back to the Catholic religion again. These peasant people, those who had no choice as their homes were burned down and their families thrown out

48

on the roadside because they could not pay the rent, also the ones who left their little cottage homes, left all their belongings, bits and pieces of furniture etc, and travelled many days to ports such as, Cork, Limerick, Tralee, to try and get passage to the U.S., Britain, Canada, anywhere that would give them hope of a new start.

Travelling the long journey from their homes had to be done on foot and the only sustenance available to them was what was called, the "Hungry grass." This grass grew stronger and higher than ordinary grass and its seed was much larger, so as they struggled on their journey they picked the seed from its stalk into a bowl and added some water. In the evening they would light a fire and warm this potion, and this, although it gave many dysentery, helped them to survive the journey.

Disease and starvation were killing so many, and emigration was sucking the life blood from our nation that the "Times of London" Wrote an obituary of the Irish Nation that read,

"That soon an Irishman in his native land,
Would be as rare as an American Indian in his."
Thanks be to the Good Lord it never came to this.

Some of the Landlords who wanted to get their tenants off the land, offered to pay their fare to the U.S. Again many were more than glad to avail of this offer, after all how could they otherwise leave this desolate land. In their wildest dreams they could never hope to come up with enough to pay their way. To think of a new life in the land of the dollar they had heard so much about, gave them a lot of hope of a good future for their families. When they arrived at the place of departure they were herded into holding stations, given some food and drink until the ship would be ready to sail. It was then that they were told that they would not be going to New York but to New Orleans. The fare at the time was £3.10s to New York and £3.oo to New Orleans, and the landlords did not want to pay the extra 10s. But the people wanted to go to New York where most already had some relations or friends, and anyhow they had never heard of New Orleans. Many had walked for a week or more to get to the ship and after hearing from the landlords and the shipping company that from New Orleans to New York was only a days' walk, decided to take the chance. In any case they reckoned it would have to be better than their present awful circumstances. Little did they know what really awaited them at the end of their voyage of hope.

When they arrived in New Orleans almost as decimated as when they had left Ireland they were indeed in a sorry state. Also witnessing the burial at sea of those who had died on the way had hugely affected them. On disembarking in New Orleans was when they heard that New York was more than 1,300 miles from New Orleans. This would be at least four times the length of Ireland, and could not possibly be done on foot. A few took control and done their best to heighten the morale of those who in their present situation had almost lost all hope of ever making good. However, they were persuaded to get organised, and try to hold on to that hope that had brought them this far. They decided that whatever, they would make the best of a bad lot, and they did. Some did get work, mostly on the docks, and helped as best they could to alleviate the suffering of all. A great barrier for most of them was the language, as Gaelic up to the time they had left Ireland, was the only tongue they knew. Of course they overcame this in time, because if one was to succeed it was a necessity to speak and understand English.

In New Orleans they were ghettoised in very poor accommodation and being from rural roots some decided to chance their luck up river. So quite a number of them left New Orleans to walk to other towns or plantations where they might get some work. Others, after somehow getting a few dollars together, took the steam boat up river to Baton Rouge, Memphis, St.Louis and other points north. Some with grit and determination to make good left their mark, and rose above their awful circumstances to survive and make a huge impact on there adopted places. I suppose that maybe at his time in the South being white would have been a distinct advantage, and some when given the position of overseer, on the Docks or Plantations, turned out to be as ruthless to the black workers as did their bosses.

Whatever the shortcomings of these people, their will to overcome and improve their lot was so strong that nothing no matter what, would stop them from going forward. Many Irish names may be found in and around the environs of St. Louis, which proves that some Irish settlers had got that far and put down roots here. Also they held steadfastly to their catholic faith and would never deny this. It wasn't easy, but they never let go.

On one occasion on a trip to the U.S. and visiting St. Louis, Missouri I pondered on the question if any of those Irish Immigrants had heard, by chance or otherwise, of the little town of St. Patrick located in North Eastern corner of Clark County in that state. This is a town settled by Irish Catholics in 1833. Its first resident pastor was of Irish stock, Fr. Denis Byrne and in 1852 it became the first organised Catholic congregation in Clark County, Missouri. It is a town in this present day of only seventeen inhabitants.

I first heard about St. Patrick from my friend Julie who lives in St. Louis and I became interested in its history. On reading up on the Great Famine, although this is not mentioned anywhere in the history of St.Patrick, and not having any evidence whatsoever, I thought maybe that some of these immigrants may have headed in that direction. So I said to myself 'let's see if I can rustle up any connection.' Having obtained a very full history of the town from Mrs Ellen Krueger of St. Patrick, who compiled this very thorough and concise research, and has written extensively about the town and its origins.

She writes,

'That the village is unique in many ways; and is the only town in the world, with a post office, named for St. Patrick the patron saint of Ireland. He is the only patron saint of the entire world. The Shrine of St. Patrick, fashioned after St. Patrick's memorial church of the Four Masters in Donegal, Ireland, is located here. It recalls in motif and design the Golden Age of Celtic Christianity. It has a round tower belfry, possibly the only one of its kind in the United States, a semi-circular recessed doorway, central rose window, Celtic crosses, and 37 stained glass windows made by the State Glass Co. of Dublin, Ireland. These windows were designed from designs found in that illuminated book of the four gospels the Book of Kells. This book is on public exhibition in Trinity College, Dublin. The interior marble is from Spain and Italy. The granite exterior was quarried in Lannon, Wisconsin. A flagstone from Ireland is imbedded in the floor in front of the altar because Fr. O'Duignan wanted to stand on a piece of Ireland as he celebrated Mass. The Shrine was dedicated by Fr. O'Duignan on March 17th 1957.

An Irishman by the name of Fr. McMenomy named it, Dempsey Highway, named after another Irishman Fr. Dempsey leads you to the village, and an Irishman Fr. O'Duignan put it on the map and made it famous. Fr. O'Duignan also designed the shamrock cachet for March 17th letters. Tommy Murphy, Ballina, Co. Mayo, Ireland, is its Honorary Mayor.'

If one would like a specially designed envelope from the shrine of St. Patrick that will include stamp, special post mark, St. Patrick's Day greeting card, and the shamrock cachet cancelling stamp, the cost is $1.oo. Of course one must remember that the cost and postage would be a little more when sent to someone outside the U.S. All proceeds from this venture go to the upkeep of the shrine. This cachet was designed by Fr. Francis O'Duignan in 1936.

Church volunteers will address the envelope, write your return address, sign the card with your name and mail them on what ever day you request between March 1st and March 30th each year.

You may choose from any of seven postcards of the shrine of St. Patrick which are:
*St. Patrick stained glass window.
*Greetings from St. Patrick, Missouri.
*St. Patrick Statue. [Outside]
*St. Patrick Statue. [Inside]
*Shrine of St. Patrick in summer.
*Shrine of St. Patrick in winter.
*Shrine of St. Patrick.

So if you would like to know more about this little bit of Ireland situated in the Northeast Missouri Hills, write or call to:
Ms. Ellen Krueger,
Route 1,
Box 55,
Canton,
Missouri, 63435 – 9637,
U.S.A.
Phone; 660 754 6028.
Official Website;
http://www.janellen.com/seasonal/stpatrick.htm
OR
www.janeellen.com

If you find yourself in the vicinity of St Patrick's some day and would like a tour of the town and shrine, write or call;
Ellen Krueger,
Publicity Chairperson,
At the above address.

In my search for evidence that some of our famine emigrants may have reached the town of St. Patrick, I failed. I have never been out in that neck of the woods and to research something from a distance of 4,000 or 5,000 miles I reckon is nigh impossible. Although at over 73 years old and time may not be on my side, I am still hopeful of paying a visit to this 'Hallowed Place.' Maybe St Patrick one day will hear my prayer. But never mind, I was delighted to hear of this little bit of the great United States of America remembering, and still paying homage, to our patron St. Patrick. It's nearly beyond ones imagination to think of the influence that one lowly slave shepherd has had in almost every corner of the world.

Photograph of the Shrine of St. Patrick, underneath this is the cachet.

Robert Service

Have you ever really thought about poetry, and what it takes to write in verse of something that you observe, or that you feel strongly about? To be able to convey that feeling you have inside so that all, layman and scholar alike, may understand and enjoy your interpretation of that particular moment. To my mind Robert Service who wrote many poems about the lives and times of the men who moiled for gold in that hostile climate of the Canadian North West and the Klondike gold rush, was one of the great observers of that era. Having read many of Service's books and poems over a number of years, I felt I should include a short essay on his works in this book.

Service conveys through verse and his novels, that, survival in this harsh and unyielding land depended mostly on comradeship, and the reliance and support a lot of the time on others. Through his poem "The cremation of Sam McGee" from his collection of "Songs of a Sourdough" published in 1907 he really tells us of this comradeship that was built up between those brought together by the hardships of that time and place, and nothing under the sun could destroy that link. Betrayal was not a word in their vocabulary; a mans word is his bond. A line from the poem goes;

"Now a promise made is a debt unpaid, and the trail has its own stern code."

So in his own mind Service was under oath to perform the last wishes of his friend and partner Sam McGee. He put the pressure and stress to pay off this unpaid debt into a fifteen verse poem to illustrate the comradeship that had been built up between the two.

The writing of poetry is surely a great gift and each poem could be considered a condensing of some novel or other, or, of making the ordinary extraordinary. Unlike some of our modern poets, Robert Service and

55

Robert Burns, affectionately known as Bobby, wrote for the educated and the uneducated. Their poems had rhyme, rhythm, and reason, they conveyed simply the vision of the author as he or she took in the sights and sounds of what they observed around them. The simplicity of Services' writings is the key to his popularity. There is no strain on the reader to try and understand the moment, when, he may have sat down and scribbled out verse after verse on the situation as he saw it then, or, had conjured up from an overheard remark made by one of his fellow travellers.

Service was born in Preston, Lancashire, England, in 1874. In 1894 he emigrated to Canada, and was seven years stationed in the Yukon with the Canadian Bank of Commerce, in Victoria B.C. After this time he took to travelling in the U.S.A. and Mexico and led a kind of vagabond existence before returning to Europe. Here he became a correspondent for the "Toronto Star" reporting on the Balkan wars of 1912 – 1913, and was a reporter and Ambulance driver during the First World War 1914 – 1918. In 1916 from his experiences in both wars he wrote "Rhymes of a Red Cross man."

His first novel "The Trail of '98" vividly conveys to the reader the conditions of mining for gold in the Klondike. From 1912 he lived mainly in Europe and had two more books published "Plough man of the Stars" 1945 and "Harper of Heaven." Some of his poems such as "The Cremation of Sam McGee" "The Harpy" and the most famous of all "The Shooting of Dan McGrew" found in "Songs of a Sourdough" published in 1957 will live for ever, as they are still very popular party pieces at weddings and other gatherings. They are recited with much gusto by the participants and received with much applause by their audience.

Robert W Service died in Lancieux, France, September 11th 1958. He was often referred to as The Canadian Kipling.

In his novel "The Trail of '98" Service gives a very striking account of the voyage from San Francisco through the Puget Sound to the frozen North, On leaving the ship, and with all their gear eventually landed on some god forsaken wharf, they headed with thousands of others for the Skagway Trail. The trek to the Klondike Valley to seek their fortune had begun, and many would perish before it would finish. This journey was fraught with danger, from the hostile land to the rotting corpses of horses and oxen strewn across the trail, and from those men and women almost out of their minds with gold fever. The thoughts of the riches that would be theirs when at last they reached the "Promised Land," was like a whipping master that drove them on regardless of the intense cold, thirst, and hunger. At this stage if necessary they would kill their mother, father, wife, husband, siblings, offspring, or any other one or thing that would threaten them with reaching their final goal.

On this trail Service had in his team some very good and reliable fellows. His closest being the one he called the "Prodigal," who maintained that when he eventually returned to his father's house he would be welcomed with open arms, and the fatted calf would be spit roasted to heighten the celebrations. Then there was Jim Hubbard, known as "Salvation Jim." This one by his own admission a blackguard and a thief had found Jesus in some hell hole of a prison, and now preached to all and sundry the error of their ways. There was also an English man knick named "The Jam Wagon," This was a general name given to an Englishman on the trail. One who cannot surely be left out is the 'Pote,' a flambuoyant dresser complete with Panama hat. He didn't claim to, but did intimate, that he came from very well bred stock, and lived entirely off his poetry. As his business card said,

"All kinds of verse made to order with efficiency and dispatch,
Satisfaction guaranteed or money back."

Whatever the occasion the 'Pote' could trot out a verse to cover it, whether it be, "Love lyrics, Memoriam odes, Ballads, or Sonnets, at very modest prices."

Camaraderie and trust was needed if they were to have the slightest chance of making the last part of the journey. When they eventually did reach the valley of gold, found a promising spot, they staked their claim as near as possible to what was called the "Mother Lode." Often by the time they got back to the claims office their claim had already being registered by someone else. It seems nothing much could be done about this, as claim jumping was a way of life for some. Service, the most observant of the lot, and although he had some luck at the mining, put pen to paper and immortalised in his many poems and books those who followed the cry of the Klondike. These came from all walks of life, tradesmen from every trade, lawyers, doctors, parsons, farmers, casino owners, hobos, prostitutes, bankers, all driven by the lure of the precious nugget. There was even a very elderly Jewish gentleman on the trail with one word in English, which he kept repeating, "Klondike! Klondike!" Some, if not most, never even reached the Land of the Midnight Sun.

In his poem "The law of the Yukon" Service writes;

"This is the law of the Yukon, and ever she makes it plain;

Send not your foolish and feeble; send me your strong and your sane

Strong for the red rage of battle; sane for I harry them sore;

Send me men girt for the combat, men who are grit to the core."

Service was indeed the master of observation and rhyme.

In my own rather limp efforts to put some thoughts together in verse I have been accused of being too dated, reminding people of that great Scottish poet

Robert Burns. Although it wasn't meant as such, fortunately for my own part I took this as a compliment, and even though Burns wrote sometimes with a very Scottish style of pronunciation, one had no problem in understanding of what Burns was trying to convey. I remember when growing up in Cork, a photographic shop in Oliver Plunkett Street, I think it was called by the name of "Happy Snaps," had a man on the footpath of the main street taking photos of pedestrians as they walked along. He would give each a ticket with a number on it. This was for the collection of the photograph in his shop in a day or two, and on this ticket was a little verse by Robert Burns that went,

"Oh what some power,
The giftie gie us,
To see ourselves,
As others see us"

Referring, of course to the wonderful works of the camera and its all seeing and unbiased eye.

Also I remember on the packet of "Sweet Afton" cigarettes, which was called after the Scottish river of that name. The name "Sweet Afton" was adopted from Burns well known ballad, "Afton Water" it went,

"Flow gently Sweet Afton among thy green braes,
Flow gently I'll sing thee a song in thy praise."

So for me to be put in the same mode as Burns, and hopefully Service, who in my estimation would be the epitome of a poet, would be a feather, and indeed a very large feather in my cap.

Christy

12.01am January 1st 1947, Christopher Joseph O'Brien arrived into this world. The first sounds he heard were the peals of the Bells of Shandon as they rang in the New Year. The midwife lifted him, turned him upside down and slapped his bum until he gave a little cry. Along with the bells, there were other sounds as well. Outside there was a brass band playing "Auld Lang's Zyne," and a loud chorus noisily singing with the band. There were other people also in the room. When he was washed and the midwife held him up for all to see, he could hear some ahhs and uhhs and isn't he beautiful. He was then given to his mother who smiled and cuddled him in to her, he felt so comfortable, and fell asleep to the sound of the band and a lot of people singing on the road outside his home.

What Christy didn't know then was that bells in all shapes, sizes and sound were to play such a big part in his life. He lived in Church Street, very close to Shandon and every fifteen minutes day and night was marked off by those bells. As he grew up, the sound of bells gave him an assuring and a very soothing feeling. Not alone from Shandon bells, but also bicycle bells, door bells, telephone bells, cow bells, alarm clock bells. Even the bells on Mick O'Neill's ferrets next door he would listen to, in the dead of night when everyone else was sound asleep.

Musical bells he loved and had several cassette tapes of those famous Austrian bell ringers. It didn't matter if the bell had a ring, a ding, a tinkle, or those with a plain old tinny sound each was music to Christy's ears.

He remembered well his first day at school. Not relishing the idea of going into this great lime stone and red brick building, he walked the short distance from home to the school, run by the Presentation Sisters.

Christy clutching tightly his mother's hand didn't know what to expect. Still clutching his mother's hand they waited in the schoolyard with what Christy in his small child's mind believed to be thousands, if not millions of other children.

Then fear and trepidation left him as a nice tall nun came out of the building and rang this great sounding brass bell. What a wonderful sound, Christy knew that from then on he would be here on time each morning to hear that beautiful sound. All the other children immediately stopped chattering, formed lines, and marched into school. When the yard had cleared Christy and his mother went in, and his mother introduced herself to some nun who took Christy away to a class room. She introduced him to the class and assigned him a desk. This would be where he would sit until he passed on to the next grade.

Going to mass on Sundays was for Christy a treat. His local church was the North Chapel as it was commonly known, its official name being the Cathedral of St., Mary and St Anne. It was also the Ecclesiastical seat of the Bishop of Cork. On the second step up to the altar was a great big, what one might call a gong. This was mushroom shaped and when the altar server hit it with this stick that had a leather covered ball on the end, the sound reverberated through the church. This happened before, during, and after the consecration. The first time Christy heard this he vowed that when he made his first Holy Communion he would become an altar server, and hit that gong so lovingly that all in the church would know that he would some day become a master bell ringer. At 6 he parted with the nuns and went to the North Monastery Primary, and the following year he received his first Holy Communion.

At eight years of age Christy was accepted as an altar server, however he wasn't allowed touch the gong until he had mastered all the other functions necessary for an altar server. He would never forget the first time the priest in charge of the servers delegated him to be the one to sound the gong at 1200noon Mass on Sunday. Impatiently he waited for the time to come, when he would for the first time, strike this beautiful brass mushroom. He felt that up to this no one had ever hit this gong with such love and reverence, and that the congregation would somehow feel this, as the sound wafted down through the church. After the consecration, and when the last gong had been sounded, Christy had the feeling that he had done such a good job, that the congregation would give him a standing ovation. The fact that he didn't get, what he thought at the time was his due, didn't phase him out one bit. In his own mind as an altar server he had reached the pinnacle of his trade.

Up to this time the priest found it hard to get servers for the 7.30am mass each week morning, but now he had no problem whatsoever. Christy volunteered to be there every morning before going to school. Rain, hail or shine, five mornings a week Christy was there, to get, if you like, his fix for the day. He was also there every Sunday, but wasn't always the one to sound the gong. On Sundays this was a job that was passed around.

The years passed quickly and at 11 years of age after his Confirmation passed into the North Monastery secondary school. He still continued to serve on the altar and still loved to sound that brass mushroom.

At 15 a friend drew his attention to a notice that a recital would be given by Mr. Bernard Griffin on the church organ and carillon in St. Colman's Cathedral, Cobh. Of course Christy had heard of this famous carilloner who also as it happened, played the organ and conducted the choir in the North Chapel. After mass one Sunday Christy approached Mr. Griffin introduced himself, and explained how he longed to be a bell ringer and organist just like him. Mr. Griffin looked at him and smiled. He recognised the boy as the one, who, when he hit the gong at the consecration somehow always made it sound more spiritual. It seemed to him that when this young man hit this gong people bowed their heads and touched their breast with much more reverence. Christy asked if it would be at all possible for himself and his mother to go to St. Colman's on next Tuesday evening, to hear his recital. Christy explained that he knew it was an all ticket affair and probably in any case, he would not be able to afford two tickets. If Mr. Griffin could arrange anything for them they would get the train down to Cobh and home again when the recital was finished.

Bernard Griffin a fine human being was taken back a little by this request from such a young boy. He can never remember anyone so enthusiastic about hearing the bells of St. Colman's, or indeed any other bells for that matter. He smiled put his arm on Christy's shoulder and said,

"Christopher I am indeed flattered and would be delighted to be of assistance in this request. If your mother and you come to the cathedral on next Tuesday evening around 7.oo o'clock and ask for me, I shall be more than delighted to see that you will be accommodated in the best seats in the house."

Christy ran home and told his Mother of this news. She could not believe that her son had the courage to confront a man like Mr. Griffin with such a request, and that Mr. Griffin had responded in such a positive and nice manner. On the Tuesday evening the two of them took the train to Cobh and climbed the hill to St. Colmans. On reaching the entrance they were confronted by a couple of men who were taking tickets. His mother explained to the men about Mr. Griffin, her son, and the tickets. Putting his hand into his pocket one of the men took out an envelope, held it up and said,

"And now young man would you by any chance be Christopher O'Brien?

"Yes Sir" said Christy "That's me."

"Well young man here are your tickets, you're right up there in the reserved area, even I failed to get a seat for my wife and sons up there. There's an usher just inside the door who will show you to your seats, and enjoy the evening."

As they walked up the long nave Christy's mother wondered,

'How did her son have so much influence with Mr. Griffin?

It was a wonderful evening Christy sat mesmerised as Mr.Griffin filled that great building with the sound of sacred and classical music on the organ and the bells. This was so much better than those tapes he usually listened to at home. This magnificent building was shook to its very foundations with the glorious sound. And to cap it all off, Mr. Griffin announced that the last piece would be played for a dear friend of his,

"Christopher O'Brien from Church Street, Cork, and in this young mans honour the recital would finish with the "Banks of my own lovely Lee."

The Cathedral resounded to the hundreds of voices of the congregation singing the Cork anthem "The Banks." When it finished, the congregation all stood up, and gave Mr Griffin a standing ovation. Truly a great end to a wonderful evening.

On the way home the noise of the other late night passengers could not invade the silence pervading between Christy and his mother. Both were in a state of ecstasy entirely oblivious of their surroundings. Neither said a word until they got home and his father asked how things had gone.

"You know." Said his mother "We've been to heaven and back."

She then motioned Christy up the stairs to bed.

After this experience his mother made some enquiries at the School of Music about a course in church organ and carilloning. All was explained to her, as regarding cost, time involved for the pupil, and the number of years it would take before any progress could be seen. The most of the first two years would be taken up with theory, and the learning of music, with very little actual organ or carillon playing. When she arrived and told Christy about her inquiries she said,

"Christy if this is what you want we'll get the money somehow."

The following week he and his mother went to the School of Music and Christy was enrolled. His father who liked a few pints most evenings after work was asked to forego this, a couple of times a week. He would he said be delighted to do this, and cut down to a quart on Saturday night, and a quart on Sunday morning. After all, if this were all the sacrifice he was to make to stop his son from becoming, what he considered himself to be, a wage slave, he would willingly do anything.

One of the things his mother insisted on was that Christy had to give up the 7.30am mass each morning. He would be soon studying for the Leaving Certificate and with three evening classes each week for music he would need all the rest he could get. He agreed with this.

Surprise! Surprise! One of the books to read for the leaving was "The Hunchback of Nortredame."

Word got out that Christy was studying by night to be a carilloner and organ player, and Christy became known to his classmates as "Quasimodo O'Brien." He didn't mind, he knew there wasn't any malice in this. As a matter of fact he considered it a compliment. After reading the book he hoped that one day he would travel to Paris, and ring those bells in the Cathedral of Nortredame. After finishing his Leaving Certificate and his music studies and getting very good marks in both, he was awarded a three year scholarship to study church organ and carillon music at Berkley College, California.

His mother was beside herself with happiness, and of course also a little sad at the thought of Christy leaving home for foreign places. Especially a place so far away. Although only 19 she felt that her son had a good head on his shoulders, and would not be easily lead from the path he had chosen. She had written to her sister who lived a short distance from Berkley, and she would look after Christy until he found his feet over there. After enrolling he quickly got a job four evenings a week in a bar and restaurant. Although the wages were small the tips were good, and now sharing accommodation with two others he could manage away fairly well.

Christy loved California so different to Shandon Street and its environs. At Berkley he really, as they would say at home, "Put his nose to the grind stone" he studied hard, got very high grades and graduated with a degree in Sacred Music. He had made a lot of friends at Berkley and was very sad to leave. Berkley had been very good for him, and he hoped he would return again some day to renew the friendships he had made while studying there.

At home he was offered a temporary position in the Cork School of Music as tutor in Hammond organ. The stipend from this would enable Christy to continue to study for his B.Mus.,

Continuing to live at home in Church Street helped him a lot financially. His parents though now getting on in life were more than delighted to still help all they could. He met with Mr. Griffin one evening in the North Chapel. Mr.Griffin was very happy with the progress Christy had made, and called him, "My protégé." He invited him to Shandon just across the road to play the bells some evening. Also he said,

"Christopher you might like to play the organ in the church some Sunday at Mass."

With this invitation Christy felt he really had arrived. To play the bells in Shandon, and to play the organ in the North Cathedral would be to date the highlight of his career. He knew he had along way to go yet to be recognised nationally, not to mind internationally as a carilloner and church organist. Of course the biggest stamp of approval would be, to be invited to play the bells and organ at St. Colman's Cathedral, and he hoped the invitation would come some day.

He had made many friends in the music business and mostly, as well as working with them, these were also the people he socialised with. So as a member of this very tight circle he very much looked forward to the future.

Being so well known in the district and when it was made known that Christy O'Brien was to be the organist at 12.oo noon Mass on the Sunday morning most of his neighbours and friends attended this Mass. Bernard Griffin conducted the choir, and when the Mass ended the priest thanked them, the congregation stood up, turned around, looked up to the organ loft and gave a loud round of applause. Christy's mother wept openly and it gave his father all he could do to hold back the tears. People came across the church to congratulate them, and they felt all the little sacrifices they had made down through the years had been well worth the effort.

Christy thanked Mr.Griffin for the faith he had shown in him and the opportunity he had given to him this morning, to show the people of his own parish that all his years of study had not been in vain. He looked forward to the future with hope and also thanked the Lord for the wonderful parents he had been blessed with, he could never have made it without them.

Our Friend Jack. R.I.P

Jack Downey, a man of many parts, also a man of many, many friends. He was first and foremost a family man, then a very skilled Tour Coach Driver, who was very happy in his job, and took great pride in his work. Jack loved meeting people and in his nearly 40 years with Cronin's Coaches he met up with people of every nationality and every walk of life, making hundreds of friends on the way. I have yet to meet anyone who had a bad word to say about Jack. He knew every nook and cranny of this country. No matter where one went in Ireland, as soon as it was known that you were a Cronin's driver you were bound to be asked,

"How is Black Jack keeping? I haven't seen him with a while."

When finished in the evening time and after the dinner, Jack liked to relax and have a couple of pints before retiring for the night. When his pint of Murphy's was served up to him it had to be dead flat, not the smallest sign of a head. This was how he liked it, and this was how he got the name "Black Jack."

I suppose in his own way Jack was unique. In his nearly 40 years with Cronin's Coaches driving visitors or locals, there was never even one complaint came in to the firm about Jack. He was funny, amicable, polite, and generous to a fault. When through his illness he was unable to attend our staff Christmas dinner, his employer Dermot Cronin spoke so highly of him as a person, a driver, a raconteur, and friend. A speech everyone present felt was a well deserved tribute to one who had served the company so well.

At times, not many I might add, Jack would get mad over something. This never lasted very long, he would stop and laugh heartily, and give us a few bars of "The Boys of Kilmichael" or another favourite of his was the ballad of "Roddy MacCorly." On top of everything else Jack was a nationalist who dearly loved his country. This was one of the reasons why he loved to drive people and show off his beautiful Emerald Isle.

When Jack succumbed to his illness on January 27th 2007 we found it so hard to believe that our friend and colleague had passed away. His removal and funeral also bore witness to the esteem in which our beloved friend was held. Every county in Ireland, North, South, East, West, was represented, and one colleague travelled from Norway to accompany Jack on his last Journey.

I'm sure it must have been a great consolation to his family that so many came to pay their respects to Jack. A wonderful Husband, Dad, Granddad, and someone whom it was a pleasure to have known and worked with.

Seán Dubh a Chara,
"Air dheis lámh Dé go raibh do anam."

Ode to "Black Jack"

A coach lies idle in the yard,
"Jack where are you?"
A high stool empty and waiting,
"I wonder where Jack is.?"
A vacant bed in the ward tonight,
"Jack's late!"
A more comfortable one in Heaven.
Jack, welcomed to your new home
By familiar faces,
Some that time may have dimmed,
But not forgotten.
Renewing old acquaintances,
Greaney, Dowling, Peter, Joan,
Smiling broadly with hands outstretched,
And caressing you lovingly,
As only old friends can do.
A flat pint held out by Greaney,
What better way to greet you Jack?
Greaney, and all those long lost friends,
Waiting patiently, to sit and talk,
As you sip the headless elixir.
While Angels, Saints, and the Lord himself,
Settle down to hear tales funny and sad,
And listening in awe,
To one talking with much gusto,
And telling it like it is about those left behind.
"Jack our friend I hope you know how much you are
missed."

All at Cronin's Coaches.

30th January 2007

The Breadman

My father, a typical droll West Cork man came to the City with one of his brothers around the 1930s. They got a job fairly quickly on the trams, my father as a conductor and my uncle as a driver. They were happy enough at this job but the pay not being great, they decided that in their off time they would put some of the skills they had learned back in West Cork to good use. So they rented a shed out in Blackpool near the old distillery. They figured that this was the ideal location for their new project as the aroma from the distillery would be more than enough to cover up the sweet smell from their entrepreneurial effort. So they proceeded to make that famous and illicit West Cork brew "Poteen." Business went very well for awhile and it showed a good profit. There was no publicity as such, only word of mouth from one satisfied customer to another.

People with Arthritis, or other pains and aches, the greyhound men, the harrier men, those with lame horses, and some others who didn't need any excuse, all became regular customers. My father had a saying about Poteen;

"Throw away your oul' pills,
It will cure all your ills,
Be you Protestant, Catholic, or Jew."

Things went very well for about three months, however nothing lasts forever and a good friend and customer of his, a sergeant in the guards, tipped him off about a possible raid, and he flew the coop. In one night they cleared out the shed and sold off all the equipment to a farmer in the Shehy Mountain area of West Cork. If the Guardaí ever did raid the shed they never bothered to find out.

He then gave up the trams and bought a horse and a covered in cart, and started his own country bread round. He sold bread, flour, groceries, the daily newspaper, and other household commodities. From the farmers he would buy butter and eggs or rabbits, and sell them to the city stores the following morning. Sometimes in Glanmire he would buy a Salmon which would have been poached in the nearby Glashaboy River. This would have been another thing the authorities would be interested in.

Of course he also brought all the gossip of the countryside, brought the news of births, marriages, and deaths. I remember one woman who loved to hear the misfortunes of others asked him: did he hear about so and so's daughter and my father said;

"Yes I hear she's pregnant."

This woman came back with;

"And that's not all Mr. Mac, did you know, she's expecting a baby as well. May God forgive her, her people must be mortified."

At that time people didn't have a lot of money and some found it very hard to pay for their weekly necessities. Again deals were made, and payments for his services were often made in kind. I remember when he arrived home with a calf, another time two Bonham's, a pair of kid goats, four ducklings, a brace of pheasants. These are only some of the things that ended up in our home on Quaker Road. All these were payment in kind for services rendered. He being a man from the west, and as far as he was concerned, the odd trade in barter was fine.

Anyway to get to the sting in the tail; this particular woman who's husband worked in the city for Cork Corporation had run up a fairly big bill with him. Her husband, poor man, cycled the eight miles to and from the city each day. Now at that time £15.oo would be considered a big bill and when she approached my father to get her weekly groceries he asked her about paying something off the outstanding bill. She started a whole rigmarole about first Holy Communion and Confirmation clothes and finished with;

72

"Mr Mac I'm sorry I haven't any money for you this week, but next week Mick will be drawing his holiday pay and Mr. Mac I promise, you will be the first in line."

And he gave her another £3.oo worth of groceries on credit. She went back in home praising the Lord, and drawing down the blessings of all the Angels and saints in Heaven on my father. My father, who was in his own way a very religious man, I'm sure would much rather if she had given him a few bob off her bill.

On the next night he called as the horse stopped outside her door, she was out like a shot rubbing the tears from her eyes with her apron, she exclaimed.

"Oh Mr. Mac, Mr. Mac, You'll never believe it, you'll never believe what happened to poor Mick on his way home from work this evening. Mr. Mac he's shook to the core."

"My God Bridie what happened Mick? Was he hit by a car or a truck? Was he hurt? Did he fall off his bike, or what?"

This was the time the steam trains used to run from Cork to Cobh and Youghal, and from the station they would run over the bridge that crossed the main road, and then run parallel with the Lower Glanmire Road.

"Oh Mr.Mac! Thank God and all his angels and saints he's O.K., but he had a very narrow escape coming down the Lower Road and under the Railway Bridge on his way home. Oh! The poor, poor man. Well Mr. Mac, As Mick was going under the bridge on his bike; the train was going over the bridge on its way to Cobh or Youghal. Just at that moment the fireman happened to be stoking the fire, and low and behold didn't a spark fly from the engine into Mick's pocket and burn his wages inside. But thank God Mr. Mac he wasn't hurt himself. Only for the grace of God Mr. Mac I'd be a widow right now."

"So Mr. Mac if I could just have two pair of bread, a pound of butter, half pound of tea and a dozen eggs I'll clear the lot next week."

I think my father felt that for entertainment value alone she was worth the risk until next week.

Cranking up the motor

For our family 1950 was the year of the car. That year our father bought a Morris Minor car of doubtful age, but if looks were to be believed, to us it was in prime condition. I needn't tell you the man he got it from had washed it, and cleaned up the inside before he parted with it. Times were hard then and the man who owned the car was a small farmer at desperate odds to feed and clothe his young family. Although his bill for bread and groceries was only £16.oo he had no hope of paying it off, and the old car, apart from his home, was really the only collateral he had. He asked my father if he would take the car in lieu of the money he owed him. After some negotiations they came to an agreement and that's how we became the owners.

The following Sunday with me on the cross bar of his old bike he cycled out to Knockraha to pick up the car. The engine was running when we arrived, they talked for a while, shook hands and the deal was clenched. I would say by the hint of a smile on his face, that farmer reckoned he had made a good deal, and was glad to see the back of that car. So with my father driving the car, and me on the bike coming in some time behind him, we arrived home to Quaker Road.

Although it had one bald tyre, the spare wheel wasn't bad but it was in the boot flat. So our pride and joy had three fairly good tyres and when the one in the boot would be repaired we felt that it would pass any test. Anyway, this didn't matter much, we had a car and we were the envy of our street. My father at that time was a travelling bread and grocery salesman and had a small Ford van on the road. He would travel around the countryside five days a week. Along with selling bread and groceries, he would collect butter and eggs to sell to the wholesalers in Cork.

When the Morris Minor was parked outside the family home someone of us were bound to pull the room curtains aside and gaze in wonder at the chariot outside our door. Just to be on the safe side the front wheels were always turned into the kerb. We did live on a bit of an incline you know, and we felt it was better to be safe than sorry. Also the hill proved a big asset when it came to starting the vehicle as we soon discovered the battery wasn't all that good. We put this down to the fact that of late it may not have been used too often. However the local garage would put it on charge for a few hours and that would fix that problem. When the battery was charged, so as not to waste its power, one would turn the wheels out from the kerb, put the car in second gear, and let it run a short distance down the hill. The engine would turn and with a couple of mighty backfires would burst into life. This usually brought some of our neighbours to their front doors to wonder what all the shooting was about. In time they got quite used to this and ignored it.

A starting handle also came with the car. This would have been about three feet long, made of steel, with a small piece protruding from each side of the tip. When the car was on the level and refused to start this tool was put into use, pushed through a hole in the bumper it engaged with the crank shaft. First making sure the car was not in gear and the petrol choke was in the out position. Then one hand was put on the bonnet to steady oneself, and the other was used to turn the crank shaft with the starting handle as quickly as possible. This was not a job for the fainthearted as it was not easy to turn the crankshaft with this tool. It might take up to ten crankings before it would eventually start. Hopefully with this manoeuvre the engine would start. If not, we all gathered around and gave it mighty push. It would give a couple more backfires before it eventually started. When it started the choke would be pushed in and again hopefully the engine would idle away on its own. It didn't have any

76

indicators either and when one wanted to turn right you put your hand out the window. When you wanted to turn left you put your hand out the window and with your hand made a circular motion.

The fact that there were six of us kids, my father and mother, and the car being a four seater didn't faze us one bit. We felt there was plenty of room for the eight of us. At that time there were three who could drive, our father, my brother a couple of years younger than me and myself. Our father already had a small Ford van that he travelled around the country with, selling bread and groceries and collecting butter and eggs. Although neither my brother nor I had a licence to drive we had learned to drive on this vehicle which was a little larger than the Morris Minor. Of course we couldn't wait to get our hands on the Morris, but as yet, the drivers' seat was forbidden territory. I didn't have a license and he was too young.

After a short time I went to the Licensing Office and procured a driving license, no problem. There was no such thing as a Provisional License then, and no driving test either. At seventeen one would present one self at the office with ones birth certificate and for £1.oo you had your license. This license allowed you to drive any sized vehicle. I can't remember how I managed to get the £1.oo together, that was a lot of money back then. I reckon it took a hell of a lot of saving, as my parents could definitely not afford to fork out £1.oo. They were delighted when I told them, but I had to give an account to them on how I managed to get a whole £1.oo together.

One Sunday after dinner my father called me and said,

"Young fellow let's go for a spin in the car, and maybe you might like to drive it for a few miles when we get out in the country."

This was unbelievable; it was as if all my birthdays had come together. I didn't have to be asked twice. Before we left he explained about the gear box being the same as the van was in the form of a "H." The position of the handbrake was different, but the clutch, brake, and accelerator were the same.

Out we headed west and at Victoria Cross we changed seats. Just sitting in the driving seat I felt that now I was an adult, and from now on I would be due a little more respect from the rest of the clan. Two of my sisters and the elder of my two brothers came along for the spin.

As I drove out the Carrigrohane straight road that evening, the only car on the road, I felt like a millionaire. I could feel the hair on my neck tingling from the envious looks of my brother. Everyone walking along the footpath, and there were quite a few, looked as we sailed along doing every bit of 25 miles an hour. Then my father said,

"Come on young fellow give her another bit of the boot."

I pressed the accelerator a little and my God I could not believe it, the speedometer needle rose to 30 miles an hour. At the end of the straight road I had to slow down somewhat and we turned left to go back in the Model Farm road. This was a different kettle of fish altogether. At that time the Model Farm road was just a narrow twisting boreen. Keeping a brave face I thought what will happen if I should meet another car coming in the opposite direction? Will we have room enough to pass? We did meet a couple of cars but thankfully they didn't pose much of a problem.

As we entered the narrow Inchigaggan Bridge to my dismay and fright, in from the opposite end came a bus. From where I was sitting it looked as if that bus was taking up the whole width of the bridge. What was I to do? Believe it or not, in panic I closed my eyes, pressed the accelerator and sailed past while waiting for the big bump that never came. My father, not knowing that I had closed my eyes, was full of praise for the way I had successfully negotiated the situation. If he had got a fright or not I do not know, as he never mentioned if he had.

On we travelled through Dennehys Cross, to Denroches Cross, down Barrack Street, along Evergreen Street, down Quaker road and parked outside our home. All the family arrived out to greet us and I was for a while the center of admiration.

Each Sunday during the summer we went, as we always called it, for a spin. One Sunday we even ventured as far as Youghal and spent the day frolicking on the beach. Although we had been here before in the van or on the train this was for us a new experience. As seat belts were unknown at that time we found that if we actually arranged ourselves in a certain way we could all more or less see where we were going.

Then, I suppose the inevitable happened; it wasn't going to go trouble free for ever. First the gearbox started slipping out of second gear, and then out of third. The engine was spluttering a bit, burning more oil than it really should and the tyres at this stage were definitely looking the worst for wear. Our local garage estimated that outside replacing the tyres it would cost around £35.oo to repair. At that time this was serious money and our parents could not afford to lash this much out. My father made a deal with the owner of the garage and he gave my father £15.oo for the car. The day he took it from our door was indeed a very sad day. We all looked out the window as our chariot slipped out from the kerb and down Quaker Road. We heard for the last time the sound of it's backfiring as it started on the fall of ground The sound that up to now had been music to our ears, now sounded to us more like the last post.

It mightn't have been much, and although it wasn't with us all that long, we kids loved it. For us this was the end of an era. Over the years we had bigger, better, and more modern cars, but none ever got the love that our Morris Minor got.

I sometimes wonder whatever became of it.

Shakespere at Feis Mathiú

Shakespeare a man in a bonnet,
Was a great one to write up a sonnet,
He wrote them with ease,
And the judges he'd please,
And they said to him,
Shakespeare you've won it.

Noahs Ark

When Noah was told of the flood,
He took himself off to the wood,
To his wife he said "Please'
While I cut down some trees,
Would you go and stock up with some grub."

Tribunal Blues

When yer man stood up in the Dáil,
He said that he could not recall,
The amount in the pot,
Or from where it was got,
'Cos I really know nuttin' at all.

Our Neighbour

Today a lady called, a friend and neighbour actually. You know the type she comes in, sits down, has some tea, and smokes and gossips for the duration. Today was something different she didn't go on with the usual gossip about some happening or scandal in our neighbourhood. It was a beautiful day and Eunice said,

"Good afternoon Betty, what a beautiful day, a good day to be alive."

Went straight out to the patio lit up a cigarette, and waited for Betty to bring out the tea. When Betty arrived with the tea and scones, after the usual chatter about the weather, each other's health, and the family, Eunice opened up.

"You know Betty," she said "While rummaging through a box of old photographs yesterday I came across a picture of yourself and Mike. You're sitting at a table, I would say in a hotel or restaurant, having a meal and you look so different. Neither one of you is wearing glasses; Mike has a head of hair many men would kill for. It's shoulder length and has a middle crease. Betty you have your hair permed and also shoulder length, let me tell you this, you both looked so cool and relaxed. You look like what some would call a golden couple. It could be at a dinner dance or some other function, there is also another couple with you whom I don't recognise. You are all dressed up to the nines."

Betty jokingly exclaims.

"Eunice don't you think we are still a golden couple?

"Well Betts I know you are and I also know that I'm not the only one who thinks this. If I'm here when Mike comes in from work I notice the way he smiles at you his eyes full of love and gives you a peck on the cheek. Then, he was never embarrassed to kiss you in public he never shied away from showing his love for you. Anyone could see after all these years he loves you very much and he's so happy to be home with you. Of course you're still a golden couple."

"As you know Eunice we celebrated our Golden Wedding Anniversary two weeks ago, and that's a half century together. We were three years together before that, and that's fifty three years altogether. Don't you think that's a lifetime? It's all past so quickly, that it seems just like it was yesterday. Mind you it hasn't all been bliss we've had our ups and downs. Times weren't always as affluent as they are now, but we and our eight children survived Thank God. Of course we were lucky in the sense that Mike never shirked work, and as a dock worker his money was always pretty good. We were never what you might call really short and those kids never went without the essentials. They always had enough food, clothing, and a roof over their heads."

"You're right of course he was never idle, always a great provider, and also never demanding. It must have been hard at times Betts, with eight kids to feed and clothe on one mans wages. And now Thank God you are reaping what you sowed. You were always there to put them out to school each morning, and when they returned in the evening you were there to welcome them home. I remember Thursday nights were very special in this house, that was the night Mike got paid and that was the night each one got his or her choice from the chipper. Betty you're both a perfect example of a marriage made in heaven. With all your ups and downs and now with all the kids having left the nest the house is so quiet, but then you are so happy in just each other's company. You are so happy together that sometimes I feel like I'm intruding.

"I'm sorry if at times you feel like this, because Eunice I think Mike feels like I do and I assure you we have never consciously meant to make you feel this way. You are always welcome here."

"I know that Betty, Thank you for saying it. I wonder who the other couple in the photograph are." Eunice said producing the photograph.

Looking at the picture Betty exclaimed,

"My God that picture must be about 50 years old, we weren't long married. How do you have that photograph? That was taken upstairs in the Arcadia, the four of us were having a cup of tea and a cake; I'd hardly recognise Jim Casey and his girlfriend of the time Agnes Murray. Actually they split shortly after that and went their separate ways. Jim I remember went to the United States and was killed in a building site accident. He was there about three years when the accident happened. He's buried out in Boston. Agnes was very upset when he left and never even got a card at Christmas from him. At the time Agnes thought he was the love of her life, but she got over him. Down in the Gresham Rooms at a Céilí one night she met this man from West Cork, married him, and lived happily ever after, I hope. He came from down around Bantry I think, or at any rate he was from back west. I haven't heard hide or hair of her since."

"Betty I remember the Gresham Rooms down in Maylor Street. On account of the big crowd that attended these dances, we called it "The "Crushums." Tuesday nights were the best if you remember, that was the nurse's night, and there would be loads of fellas in from the country. Yes that was one of the most popular nights of the week. Thompson's Bakery in McCurtain Street would have a dance in the Gaiety up near the Collins Barracks once a week as well. That was great craic also. The A.O.H. Hall on Morrison's Island another great venue as was Francis Hall up near the Mardyke.

The Arcadia on Saturday night was the best of all. Remember the big English bands that would be there on Saturday nights. Sid Phillips, that drum crazy Eric Delaney, Humphrey Lyttleton, Joe Loss, our own Michael O'Callaghan and there was so many others I just can't remember off the top of my head, and what about the Showbands they were something else. The Clipper Carltons, the Dixies, the Royal, the Capitol, the Arrivals and more too numerous to mention. Dolly Butler, who played the piano and her band with singer Danny McNamara or Perry Leahy would nearly always be the support band to all these big names. 2.oo O'clock in the morning it would be over, and then at that time we'd attend 2.30am mass in St. Patrick's on the way home and sleep our brains out on Sunday. This mass, if you remember, was especially for the pilgrims who would be heading for Knock on the early train, and what a Godsend it was to us, as the song goes Betty;"

'Those were the days my friend, I thought they'd never end.'

"Well Betts nothing lasts for ever, but definitely they were the good old days. And another thing, there was no alcohol involved either. We were quite happy if some guy would either buy us a cup of tea and a slice of Swiss Roll, or just an orange juice. If you got as we used to say 'A Walk' that's what it meant. It didn't mean that you had to jump into bed with him when you reached home. After a short stall in the dark corner by Jones house and a few kisses you sent him back, probably to the other side of the city, to his mother. Maybe, if he was your type and had a good job, you'd make a date for the Gresham Rooms for the following Tuesday night."

"Eunice what about the Tango King? Bernie something or other I can't remember his Sir name. Every girl in the hall wanted to dance with him, but, it wasn't every girl in the hall he'd dance with, he had his favourites. With his velvet jacket, his tight pants, black patent leather shoes and his quiffed Brylcreamed hair as my grandmother would say: 'wasn't he the rael lad?' I heard he died in England a few years back. God rest him."

"And Jimmy Smith, Betts wasn't he the best jitterbugger you ever saw; my God he could throw you from one end of the hall to the other and be there before you to pick you up again. Remember the night my sister Lucy was dancing a slow waltz, we used to call it a clinger, with the Scots fellow in the kilt. He was holding her real close and she thought he was getting a bit too randy and said to him;

"Come here boy would you ever take that thing out of the way?"

And he says to her,

"Acht that's all right lass, that's just ma Sporran"

She got real cross and said;

"Look boy I don't care what you call it, just get the thing out of the way."

"I remember it well, sure weren't we all laughing over it for a week. Poor Lucy she had to put up with a lot of slagging over that. My, my Eunice look at the memories one old photograph has churned up. Things I thought the years had completely obliterated from my mind. It's nice to reminisce and remember that once we too were young. Now sit there and have another smoke while I go in and boil up the kettle, and then we'll talk some more."

State of the Nation

Two old friends Mikey and Mossie after leaving the employment stand on the Cork docks walk as far as the canteen on Connell Street sit down with a mug of tea each and have a chat with some of the other Dockers. Most of the talk is centered on the lousy weather, the Ireland soccer team and their display against Cyprus the previous night, the replacing of the present manager, and speculating on who would be the best one to replace Steve Staunton. As usual the best selectors were at this present moment gathered around a table in this canteen. Each had his own favourite but the general consensus did favour the local great, now manager of Sunderland, idol Roy Keane.

The morning is rather wet and the only work they could get was on a timber boat discharging bales of timber. This meant that they would be on the quay side all day and when the crane landed the bales from the ship on to the quayside they would remove the wire lifting ropes from the crane hooks. The forklift trucks would then remove the bales and load them on to Lorries or pile them in another part of the quay. The Dockers would make bundles of the used wire ropes and these would go back into the ship when the discharging was finished. Even with the rain gear supplied, to them it was not good job. So they decided to have a few pints, do a few horses before returning home, and leave this day to the younger fellows. These younger guys could not be all that choosy.

Just now they were free and easy as each owned a mobile home in Garryvoe in East Cork, and their wives and families were on holiday down there at present. If there wasn't any work at the weekend they'd both get on a bus, as their cars were in Garryvoe, and join their families at the seaside for a day or two.

Finishing the tea they walk as far as the statue and get the no.2 bus to their local pub in Gurranebraher. Alighting from the bus near their local, they go inside order two pints, pick up a morning paper each and settle down to study form while having their couple of pints. This was a harder job than the ordinary man in the street imagined. You didn't just stick a pin in the racing page and hope for the best, one had to size up the pros and cons of each animal in each race going back over at least the last three races of each horse. Also sometimes one had to rely on ones own knowledge of a particular horse, and of course a hunch that maybe this time out this animal may be worth a bet. It certainly was a job that could not be rushed. So after about an hour, and two pints later, they made their selection. When they had the horses picked they slipped out to the bookies, just two or three doors away, to back their choices. Although they had spent an hour studying their choices, they again gave them the once over before actually putting on their money. To them gambling was a very specialised business.

Their bet was what is known as a 25c "Yankee." Picking four horses in accumulator, doubles, and trebles, with an investment of just €2.75, if the four won it would prove to be a very good investment indeed. They could take the Bookmaker for a good bit of money. It hadn't happened to any of them yet, but, they had enough faith in their system to believe it would happen some day. Coming out from the Bookies they decided to have another pint before going for home, and watch the racing on the tele for the evening. Before going back into the bar the two stand in the shelter of the doorway and have a smoke.

"Isn't a fright too Mossie that the only two things we enjoy most outside the horses, is a pint and a fag, and they won't allow us to have them together in comfort. Mossie boy their telling us all how we should live our lives, and coming up with different 'Dos and Don'ts' every other day. No wonder some call it the

Nanny State. Did you see that show "Big Brother" on the tele last night? I'll tell you Mossie boy, it has nothing on us and the way we're under scrutiny all the time where ever we go. Next they'll be putting cameras in the jacks."

"Mikey don't be so sure that there not in there already. I heard the other night on the news that some blokes and I suppose some oul' dolls too, are now using the flat top of the wash hand basin to sniff a line of coke. So what do you think of that?"

"Go away Moss I find that very hard to believe. I mean sniffin' coke in the jacks; Shur that could be very dangerous and very unhygienic as well. I'd say you picked that up wrong."

"Maybe I did, but somehow I don't think so. The youngsters today are up to every caper, they'd do anything for a high. Not like in our day Mikey, if you got a walk from the Arc, and a bit of a stall on her doorstep before she went in home you'd be on a high for a week. And if you had any bad thoughts about going any further, you were doomed. You'd have to go to confession the following day, and be lucky if you got away with five decades of the rosary for your penance, and that you weren't excommunicated for thinking and enjoying such impure thoughts. Of course if you didn't enjoy such thoughts it was O.K. My God! What innocent times we grew up in."

After finishing their smoke and are back inside sitting on the high stools again Mossie says;

"Well Mikey what do you think of our new government?"

"Ha! Ha! You call them a new government? Sure isn't it more or less the same oul' crowd are in there again. The change is, that there is no change, and what will their first move be? Their first job will be, to close down the Dáil and go on holidays for about three months. And why? Because their exhausted after the canvassing, and all that oul' rubbish and promises they've given us on the doorstep has 'em worn out.

89

Then when they'll return in September will probably vote themselves another rise. No messing, no phasing in, no going to the Labour Court for them, and always a unanimous vote. Mossie, what a shower, when we get a couple of bob rise they always tell us we're going to bankrupt the country, and leave us wait for at least six months before we actually get it. A load of sweet talkers that's all they are."

"Your right I suppose but remember Mikey they got a bad fright this time at the polls. They really thought they had nothing to do but sit back and await the will of the people, and cruise into Leinster House again. They nearly became a cropper by the will of the people, that's what they did. "

"You see Moss the people as far as I can see wanted a different crowd in, they voted for change, and messed up the whole caboodle completely. Of course not everyone understands the working of the PR system. The way the people voted this time, meant that their second and third preferences went all over the place and didn't follow the party line as in other years. I hate to say it Mossie boy, and don't get me wrong, but isn't it at times like this that the oul'. bit of education counts. Some people just don't have a clue."

"I know Mikey shur people are very stupid when it comes to election time. They vote number one with their head, and follow on then and vote the rest with their heart. Elections are like the horses. One must take time, study form, and then cast their vote."

"Exactly Mossie boy, that's it in a nut shell. Imagine where we'd be if we hadn't spent the first hour here studying form. God we'd never make a few bob. No, to study the form of the candidates is just as important as to study the form of the horses."

"You know Mikey I honestly think I'm not going to vote in any more elections. What's the use? And now we have 'How green is my valley.' It's bad enough having to go outside when you want a smoke in a pub or wherever, but, if those guys get their way they'll have

'No Smoking' signs on our garden gates. Imagine it Mikey sittin' down after the grub and your oul' doll telling you,
'You are now in a smoke free zone, if you want to smoke get out in the back yard.'
I'm telling you boy it's coming to this. It surely is."

"Moss you're quite right, it is coming to this. You know my youngest one she's paranoid about smoking, she has no smoking signs in every room and a sign in the kitchen with an arrow pointing out the back door that says "Smoking Area." And what about those green fellas and their global warming, don't mind the smoking, soon they'll be telling us we can't break wind because we are damaging the ozone layer.

"Indeed there could be a lot of truth in what you say Mikey. I read in one of the Sunday papers that even the cattle crapping in the fields may now also be a contributing factor to global warming. Now what do you think of that?

"Mossie boy not alone that, soon that crowd will have us all on bicycles, and monitoring everyone. Every farm in the country will have what you might call a Flatulent Meter, and of course these will be connected to a computer in the Ministry of Agriculture and each farm will be monitored on a daily basis. Each farmer will then have to pay a yearly levy depending on how much his herd of cattle has contributed to this global warming. What I'd like to know is who's going to monitor the monitors. Ha! The way you're smiling there Moss I know you're thinking,"
'Is this guy for real, he's only on his third pint and his imagination is gone wild?'
"Mikey it's no wonder that on the docks they call you 'Tom Pepper' and 'Ripley' you have a way for exaggerating every situation. Why don't you look around you, as far as this country is concerned where is the evidence of global warming. We're at the end of June and we must have the heating on for a bit in the evenings. April was the best month we've had so far this

year. If the ice cap is melting, outside of all that goddamn rain we're getting, we don't see much evidence of it in this country. As a matter of fact we could do with a bit of global warming around here. As far as the bikes are concerned sure wouldn't be great for getting to work in the mornings. But how would be get back up the hill in the evenings? After a days work on a bag boat or cargo boat you wouldn't have much mind for pushing your bike up the hill home. Shur by the time you'd be home you wouldn't have the energy to eat the grub. You'd be only fit for the bed"

"Yeh you're right on there, but, what's this business the Harbour Board is talkin' about now Moss? A strong rumour is going around, I'm sure you've heard it as well, that all the up river docks work will be moving down to Ringaskiddy in about two or three years. Where do you think that will leave us Mossie boy? I hope it won't, if you'll pardon me, leave us high and dry. I mean, where could you and I get another job or who do you think would employ a couple of ould codgers like us? Especially with all those young foreign guys ready, able, and willing to take whatever becomes available. We wouldn't stand a chance."

"That's what you think Mikey boy; the Harbour Board would have to take us with them. What about all our years of experience? Those guys couldn't sling timber, or steel, or cargo, or anything else for that matter."

"Mossie, don't you know well, there are so many training agencies now that it wouldn't take long to train those young and willing hands. Talking about timber I believe some Canadian crowd are now building a multi decked ship. All the timber will then be exported on trailers and will be discharged by tractor unit at its destination port. No more cranes or forklifts will be wanted. When the ship returns again with another cargo the empty trailers will be loaded on board and returned to Canada."

"Mikey boy where do you get your ideas from? That would never work here; it wouldn't be feasible because of the amount of space that all those trailers would take up ashore."

"Anyway Moss we both have nearly forty years service on the docks if this happens we would be entitled to a handy lump sum and a pension. We'd be sittin' on the pigs back, every day we could have a few pints and a few bob on the gee gees. Life would be perfect."

"I don't know all the same Mikey; I think you're running away with yourself as usual. Look at Sully; four years ago he thought he'd never see a poor day again. Now as you well know Sully was never one to spend his few bob foolishly, always with him the family came first. Unfortunately for him when he got his redundancy he opened a joint bank account, and Helen with her new found wealth didn't find Crosshaven or Garryvoe attractive anymore for a holiday. Lanzarotte and other classy places abroad was the only thing for her. Then this business of her and the two daughters going to New York for the Christmas shopping made short work of his bank account. God help us Mikey, Sully is now driving a pickup truck for some builder, and he's working twice as hard now than he ever did in the job he was in when he was made redundant. I believe he's happy enough though, he always took life kind of easy, never looked beyond today, and with the pension and the job he'll survive alright. I'd say if Helen could get to Crosshaven for a week in the Summer time now she'd be happy enough."

"Well Mossie whatever happens with the Harbour Board and our redundancy I'm going to head for home now and even though the day is inclined to brighten up I'll still stay in and watch the racing and hope we'll be cashing our dockets in tomorrow for some big money, and heading for the Seaside for a week."

"But Mikey at the same time 'God send us no greater loss' I'll head for home too, and I'll give you a shout about quarter past seven in the morning."

Draining their glasses they say good bye to the barman, and head out the door for home. Donie the barman retorts,

"Good Luck with the horses."

7.15am next morning, Mossie stands outside Mikeys gate, and gives the usual whistle, and in less than one minute Mikey joins him and off they go down the hill to work.

"God Mikey what a beautiful morning, a great morning to be alive. I see Jimmy next door to me has the pigeons out early. He's getting them ready for the big race in England next week. I hope he does well. He's a hard man you know is Jimmy, I've heard him several times talking to the pigeons especially before a big race abroad. As he's putting them in to the transporting baskets he's giving them a pep talk about how to out manoeuvre the opposition when their coming in over the Irish coast, and the shortest route home from there. That's the Gospel truth; he reminds me of that Dr. Doolittle guy, he really loves those birds. Come here Mikey, how did you do on the horses?"

"Oh! Mossy don't talk to me about them bloody horses. The first came up at 4/1 and the last one came in third at 3/1. I'll have a few bob back alright so I suppose I'll give 'em another go today. What about yourself?

"Mikey, I don't know where I went wrong yesterday, four bloody donkeys I backed. There were two I backed and they were so far behind the field I don't think there home yet. Shag 'em anyway I really thought that this docket was a sure winner. However we might be luckier today. Come here Mikey did you see that 'You're a Star' final on the tele last night? What a show, entertainment how are you. I often heard better down in Katy Barry's. That Jack O'Shea's gang that won it, my God they were awful. Jacko? He was a great

94

footballer, but as a stage bawler, I think he should think again before he gives up the day job. I saw him in the park and I saw him in Killarney, you know Moss the way he could dance around that Cork team and then round them again to score a goal or a point. He was pure magic on the field, a genius. Well last night on that stage he was like someone that had graduated from the 'Mike Murphy Academy of Dance' a pure out and out legger if ever I saw one. "

"Wisha Mossie boy shur the show was just a bit of craic, it was all for charity. You were not supposed to take it seriously. But I will say this much though, that JCB fella from the Gaeltacht made last seasons winner John Aldridge sound like Pavarotti. An out and out crow."

"Look Mikey his initials are SBB not JCB although I will give you this, I've heard sweeter sounds coming from one of Loftus' JCBs.

Right. On reaching the dock area Mossy says;

"Come on Mikey we'll have one mug of tea in the canteen before we hit the stand. There's a big bulk boat for Gouldings and a barge for the Gas Rig, so there will be no charity for them young fellas here today. We'll take our pick and as you are Moss let's get the show on the road."

The Missing Sledge Mystery

Churchfield,
Cork.

Mr. Perry O'Flaherty,
Private Investigator,
Limerick.

Dear Mr. O'Flaherty,
You have come very highly
recommended to me as person of extraordinary talent
in the solving of cases of theft by stealth or otherwise.
For some time now I have been missing a sledge
hammer that disappeared mysteriously from my garden
shed. Although the trail of the thief at this late stage
may be rather cold, I have no doubt judging from your
C.V., procured by me from the Labour Exchange, you
are the one on which I should pin my hopes of the
recovery of the aforementioned tool.

I have my own suspicions, and these fall
squarely on the shoulders of a very shifty looking
character from Brooklyn, New York, who also happens
to have a small estate not far from Limerick City. This
guy while visiting my home some time ago went
scrounging around my garden shed, and above all the
junk contained therein he showed quite an interest in
my sledge hammer. Of course I cannot name him in
print just yet, fearing he might have grounds to bring a
libel case against me. If it does indeed turn out that he
is the one I'll surely wipe the court house floor with
him. Mr. O'Flaherty please let me know if you will take
my case, and if so, what your retainer will be. I will let
you have same by return post.

You may wonder why someone should bother to
hire a person of your calibre just to find a missing
sledge hammer. Well Mr. O'Flaherty this is no ordinary
sledge hammer. It has been in my family for 4
generations and is of great sentimental value. My Great

Grandfather bought this particular hammer on a fair day in the town of Dunmanway, Co. Cork, in 1881 and all that has ever been done to this tool since, is, that it got two new heads and three new handles. So you see why I am so attached to it and am so anxious to get it back.

Hoping my request will meet with a favourable reply,

I remain yours sincerely
Sledge McHammer esq.

Mason House,
Mason Place,
Limerick.

Mr. Sledge McHammer,
Churchfield,
Cork.

Dear Mr. McHammer,

It was with great interest that I read your letter regarding your missing sledge hammer. I guarantee that you sir have contacted the right man. I am probably the worlds' greatest detective, and, scanning through my C.V. you will have noticed the number of cases I alone have solved. When others have cried, "I haven't been hired in time the trail is gone cold." I sir, have stepped into the breach and won the day.

Well Mr. McHammer as you see, I specialise in cold cases like yours, and I'm sure I'll have your sledge back to you in no time at all. Just now I am at a loose end and will be able to give your case my full attention. My fee will be €25.oo per working hour plus expenses, with a retainer of €300.oo up front. I must have this before I start, as at the moment my own bank balance is rather a little embarrassing to me. If this is O.K., with you I will start immediately on your case.

Regards,
Perry O'Flaherty, P.I.

P.S. I'm also thinking that your name Sledge McHammer may be a "non de plume." Please let me know if this is so.

P. O'F.

Churchfield,
Cork.

Mr. Perry O'Flaherty P.I.,
Limerick.

Dear Mr. O'Flaherty,
  I am humbled, flattered, and
delighted that a man of your ability has seen fit to take
my case. Although I am a man of limited means, I will
gladly accept your terms and will enclose a cheque for
€300.oo. Having said this I will expect you to give this
case your full attention and expertise. I will not tolerate
laxness on your part. If at any time during your
investigation you happen to meet up with this Brooklyn
fellow be very careful. He is such a smooth talker that
even a person of your calibre could be easily taken in by
him. Be on your guard at all times.
  I do not know why you should think that I am
using a "Non de Plume" as "Sledge" is a name given to
all first born males in our family. Over many
generations some of my ancestors have worn this name
with great pride. Have you not heard of that great
General Sledge McAmma who with the Duke of
Wellington by his side put paid to Napoleon at the
Battle of Waterloo?"
  I will end by saying "Good Hunting."

Sledge McHammer esq.

Mason House,
Mason Place,
Limerick.

Sledge McHammer esq.,
Churchfield,
Cork.

Dear Mr. McHammer,

I am in receipt of your cheque for €300.oo and indeed very grateful for your quick response, as I'm sure you realise that every minute counts. Really Mr. McHammer I am a little intrigued by this case and I can see from the history of this tool that its return is a priority. I can see that, as well as its sentimental value, in this case its historical value must also be taken into account. It is a family heirloom and in you and your family's opinion probably bordering on the priceless.

Be assured Mr McHammer that your case is in the best possible hands. At the risk of losing my reputation as the Worlds greatest P.I., I would also ask you to say three "Hail Mary's" to St. Anthony and promise him €5.oo when it's found. I'm sure between the two of us I can guarantee its safe return.

Will keep you posted,
I remain yours etc.,
Perry O'Flaherty, P.I.

Churchfield,
Cork.

Mr Perry O'Flaherty,
Mason Place,
Limerick.

Mr. O'Flaherty,

May I please have an update on how the investigation by you of my missing sledge hammer is progressing? It is now two weeks since you received my impassioned plea for the safe return of same, and need I mention also my cheque for €300.oo and not a sound from you. I am really getting quite upset, and if I may say so, I am beginning to wonder if perchance you have located my sledge hammer and are now somehow in co-hoots with this Brooklyn guy to part me from more of my hard earned cash.

It may also have turned out that this Brooklyn guy is more than a match for you. It grieves me to say this, in spite of all your credentials it seems you are no match for him. O'Flaherty I warned you to be on your guard, now I fear the worst. Another thing, about this business of St. Anthony, I'm starting to feel that I would have been better off if I had trusted more in him, and he certainly would have been a lot cheaper.

I am not given to using unseemly language, but O'Flaherty get up off your butt and start earning you money.

Sledge McHammer esq.

Mason House,
Mason Place
Limerick.

Sledge McHammer,
Churchfield,
Cork.

My Dear Mr McHammer,
Referring to your last correspondence regarding your missing sledge hammer I must say this, your assumptions in respect of my integrity cut me to the quick. May I say it is more than bordering on the libellous, never before has anyone accused me of collusion with a perpetrator of such a heinous and despicable crime. I am so incensed by your pettiness that I should by right forget about your sledge hammer, but, I feel that its missing is like a death in the family, and so I will carry on regardless of your accusations.

You were right about one thing though, this Brooklyn guy is a very clever agent, and has left bits of information here and there about your sledge hammer, making sure that they would come to my notice and which were all false. He has indeed led me a merry chase.

Do not lose hope Mr. McHammer, there is as they say a little light at the end of the tunnel, and I feel that very shortly I will have this case solved without the help of that great finder of lost objects St. Anthony. Then Sir, I will make you eat your words. Or maybe I may take a libel case against you and then we will see who is the greatest.

No regards,
Perry O'Flaherty P.I.

Mason House,
Mason Place,
Limerick.

Mr. S. McHammer,
Churchfield
Cork.

Dear Mr. McHammer,
Having failed to
locate your sledge hammer so far I have taken the
liberty of enlisting the help of a certain Mr. Sherlock
Holmes of Scotland Yard. You may have heard of him
as he is almost, but not quite, as famous as myself.

I have at long last seen this Brooklyn guy in
the local pub and although I have not spoken with him,
I can endorse your sentiments entirely. He is a shifty
looking character and a man I would say without any
qualms of conscience. Since he arrived in this area
quite a number of items have gone missing. These
include Trotting ponies, rowing boats, a mobile home,
and at least one motor lawn mower. I tried to look
around his estate in the Cratloe Hills, but could not get
any further than the electric entrance gates. These are
exactly similar to the ones missing from our Presidents
home at Árus an Úachtarán in the Phoenix Park. So
you see why I had to enlist the services of Mr. Holmes.

This Brooklyn guy is a tough cookie, but given
another week or two, Holmes and myself should have
your sledge hammer safely back to you. So if you
forward to me another cheque for €300.oo we guarantee
its safe return.

Yours in successful crime prevention,
Perry O'Flaherty.

Churchfield,
Cork.

Mr. Perry O'Flaherty,
Mason Place,
Limerick.

O'Flaherty,

Is fool written all over my letters? To me it looks fairly obvious that at last you have some inkling as to where my missing sledge hammer may be found. I ask myself is this guy holding out for more money. And the answer is 'very likely.'

I see that you have employed another to help you locate it. Well you're out of luck O'Flaherty I hired you and you are the only one who will be paid by me. Before I say any more, I feel I must inform you that the said Mr. Sherlock Holmes is not, and never was a member of Scotland Yard. This gentleman is nothing but an excuse for a private investigator. In all his life he never solved one case on his own. It was always that fine gentleman by the name of Watson, solved all the cases accredited to your Mr. Holmes. As a matter of fact Mr. O'Flaherty it is well known that the aforementioned Mr. Holmes, without Mr. Watson, could not find his way home to Baker Street. So please get him off my case immediately, I will not part with any of my money to pay him. To my mind he is every bit as big a fraud as that guy from Brooklyn, who would at the blinking of an eye steal your sledge hammer from under your nose.

It is now one week to Christmas; enough time has been wasted by you on this case. If by the New Year my sledge hammer has not been found then I will have no option but to remove you from this investigation.

Happy Christmas,
Sledge McHammer esq.

Mason House,
Mason Place,
Limerick.

Mr. S. McHammer,
Churchfield,
Cork.

Mr. McHammer,

In your last letter I see a lot of negativity in your attitude towards the handling by me of your case. I assure you, you could not be more wrong, especially about my good friend Mr. Sherlock Holmes. It was Watson who was the bungling fool who interfered with and upset Holmes' investigations at every turn. On this point I do think that an apology from you would not be out of place. However I have dispensed with Mr. Holmes and will continue to confront the guy from Brooklyn on my own. I do think I am well able to do this on my own. When I entered the public house he frequents here in Limerick he became visibly upset, finished his pint, and left in double quick time.

Now Mr. McHammer if this is not a sign that, by sheer perseverance I have worn this guy down. I believe he is on the verge of confessing and is ready to hand over your sledge hammer in the immediate future, if not by Christmas, without a doubt by the New Year.

Many happy returns,
Perry O'Flaherty P.I.

Churchfield,
Cork.

Mr. P. O'Flaherty,
Mason Place,
Limerick.

Ho! Ho! Ho! Surprise!! Surprise!! And when I say surprise, I mean SURRRRRRRRRRRRRRRRRRRRRRRPRISE!!! On awakening yesterday morning I stole silently down stairs to see what good old Santa Claus had brought me. But, alas and alack there was my stocking hanging limply from the chimney, empty. Feeling rather disappointed I looked around the room, and under our Christmas tree I saw this large and long package. I ventured nearer and could see that my name was on it.

I struggled to remove it from under the tree and the weight of the thing had me perturbed. Eventually I dragged it out on to the floor and removed the packaging. I could not believe my eyes! Mr. O'Flaherty there was this beautiful new shiny sledge hammer looking up at me. I was overwhelmed and almost struck dumb.

Who could it possibly be had written to Santa on my behalf? Or, like all good Santa's did he just happen to know what I needed most in this world? In any case I now have this sledge hammer to leave to future generations of our family. I know they will cherish and be proud of this magnificent tool, and will keep it in a safe and secure place where someone like that Brooklyn guy cannot get their greasy thieving hands on it. At this point in time the fact that Santa has broken three slates on the roof, has damaged the chimney pot, and put a big crack in our marble fireplace counts for nothing. As a matter of fact I may even mount this magnificent tool in a glass case, and place it in a place of honour over the fireplace in our living room. Here everyone who will visit will be able to gaze in admiration and jealousy at my prized specimen of a sledge hammer.

Well Mr. O'Flaherty this incident does not excuse you from your mission. Remember you are still on a retainer fee to produce the goods, and as promised by you to produce it early in the New Year, which is less than one week away. You know if my Great Grandfather, my Grandfather, or my father knew that the original sledge hammer was missing they would turn in their graves, and come back to haunt me. Now you wouldn't want that Mr. O'Flaherty, would you?

I am signing off now and withholding any more fees until my sledge hammer is safely in my possession. I am hoping that you will now get up off your butt, and finish the job you have been assigned to do. I will tolerate no more excuses.

Yours in anticipation,
Sledge McHammer esq.

Mason House,
Mason Place,
Limerick.

Mr. S. McHammer,
Churchfield,
Cork.

Dear Mr.McHammer,

At last this is the end of your sledge hammer saga. When I opened my front door this morning, there, leaning against it was your long lost sledge hammer. A surge of pride swelled my heart and nearly tore it from my body, as I gazed lovingly at the tool that nearly lost me my sanity. I had indeed won the battle and broke the spirit of that Brooklyn blackguard who came here and tried to impose himself and his dastardly ways on the good citizens of our dear country. But he reckoned without, even if I say so myself, the master.

So Mr. McHammer this tool should be in your possession in two days time. I will expect to have the rest of my fee of €300.oo by return post. We then can finally close this episode, and I will be able to give my O'Flaherty P.I. full concentration on recovering the rest of the articles stolen by this scoundrel.

Happy New Year,
Perry

Churchfield,
Cork.

Mr. P O'Flaherty,
Mason Place,
Limerick.

Dear Mr O'Flaherty,

What a great relief,
my long departed sledge hammer arrived by D.H.L
courier this morning, The poor fellow nearly had a heart
attack trying to get it from his van to my front door. I
now no longer require your services. It seems that the
pressure brought to bear on that Brooklyn fraudster
has finally paid off. From what I hear he is a completely
broken man, and the guys in the white coats are on
their way to remove him to a state or place of
punishment where he will suffer for a time, until he is
fully rehabilitated. Mr O'Flaherty with all his big talk
and all his swaggering, he could not hold out any
longer. Your final cheque is already in the post and
should be in your hands by to morrow morning.

Now that I have two sledge hammers I am
thinking of clearing out my shed and holding a yard
sale to try and recoup some of my costs this case has
set me back.

Thankfully yours,
Sledge McHammer.

Futile Love

Once again the same old story,
Yet another night of gory,
Guns are spitting, Bodies splitting,
Men are dying for love, of what?

Young men, old men, women too,
Baby's lying in their cot,
Assassin's bullet does not distinguish,
And some more have died for love, of what?

Nationalism, Colonialism,
Patriotism, Landlordism,
Put them all beneath each other,
They'll add up to naught.

Papal plea for peace rejected,
Though on bended knees 'twas sought,
Gunmen answered with automatics,
And some more have died for love, of what?

Straining 'neath its weight to Calvary,
Our salvation dearly bought,
All His agony, all His suffering,
Could it be He's died for naught?

"When will they ever learn?"

I Would Attempt Anything

With you, I want to dare anything
Even conquering the Caribbean,
And discover on your body
The firmament's geography.

To be a soldier of unwinnable battles
And leave victorious from unequal combat,
With my disfigured and messy face by bombs
But my impeccable uniform still brightly coloured,
Between dice and coloured letters
With made up dolls and stuffed animals
I'm your favourite soldier.

To be a thief of enchanted treasures
To entangle poems in your hair,
Daring the guard of pots and pans
And discovering grandma's magical recipes
To detain nightfall,
While I tell you, that this evening
Smells, of forget-me-nots, orchids and jasmines.

To be the wizard of the favourite tale
To embody the unseen
To stop, the celestial dance of thousands of
constellations
And slide from the page to your bed,
When all appears possible
Even the moon hiding between clouds
The ever lucid pen between my fingers gives in.

Twilight Zone

"Oh sweet boredom have I ever offended thee?" As I sit and sip my coffee, not really looking at, or thinking about my present surroundings, after all they have become common place, part of my daily routine. I don't know, and don't care much who these people around me are, what they do, or what they used to do, or if they've ever done anything at all. For all I care they may be just illusions as each is sitting there listening or speaking. And each even though they seem to be in deep conversation, I'm sure they would be as disinterested in the other as I am myself. Their robot like heads nodding and their robot like lips moving like zombies. The vacant look in their eyes saying they wished they could be somewhere else and with someone a little less boring.

Getting on in life and alone is really no great shakes. Let's be honest, it's probably the worst part of life. Sure you have friends, what's left of them anyway, and those that are left are just like me, waiting for Goddot. In the departure lounge, waiting for Gabriel to blow his horn and call them to the Promised Land, if there is such a place. Most of my friends have already heard the call and have gone to their just reward. Wherever they maybe I hope their very happy.

Now and then I do some thinking about this Promised Land business, and you know I discover I don't really want to leave good old planet Earth and I certainly don't want to live anywhere but in the good old Emerald Isle. At the risk of sounding blasphemous, why should I? Life has been good to me. I've been well educated, had a very good job, my pension is more than adequate to keep me in comfort, and, although I've never married I've always had plenty of friends. I did meet Miss Right many years ago and thought that this was it. A life of fulfilment, togetherness, love, marriage, and all that jazz. The only problem was, Miss Right was looking for Mr Right, and, I was not he. So, I never heard "Here comes the Bride" as I walked down the church isle my forever partner by my side. However I did have a few liaisons along the way so I'm not a complete innocent either.

However, facing into the twilight years is no great shakes, and at the same time I think,

'If the next life is anything like this one, I reckon I would be very happy.' The only thing, or so I'm led to believe, is, that this life is just a preparation for the next. The way we have lived and behaved in this life will either be good enough for us to pass through the Pearly Gates or end up somewhere where we will pay dearly for our sins. So what this means is, if I'm considered to be a good candidate, I'll more or less waltz into paradise. And one never knows I may meet miss right up there.

In a way I'm really flummoxed by all this talk about Paradise, because for me, this old Mother Earth has been Paradise. I've hardly ever been what one might call sick, all I've ever suffered from is, the odd cold or headache. Most of my friends, have at some stage in their life, been confined to hospital for a period, but me, never. Not even appendix or measles, and these are illnesses that nearly everyone suffers from early in life. Reincarnation is another thing I've been told about, and this does not appeal to me either. From what I hear one does not have a choice as to what he or she would like to return to this life as. They say that you may return as a dog, a cat, a horse, or some other animal, or even, the No. 64 bus. Now I ask you, 'Who would want that?' Whatever about the No. 64 bus, animals are definitely out. There is so much cruelty to animals one could easily end up in the wrong household. If by chance I should end up coming back as a bus, I surely hope it's a Greyhound Bus and then hopefully I would travel the U.S. coast to coast. A country I love nearly as much as Ireland.

Enough of this meandering for now here comes my friend Jack. Jack is a widower around five years or so, has a big family, seven children and numerous grandchildren, but misses his late wife so badly that sometimes I could cry for him. They were married forty three years when she passed away. It was a terrible shock to him. Hardly ever a day sick in her life, she died suddenly as they were sitting together watching television. They were having a glass of wine, their usual night cap, when, the glass fell from her hand. She lay back on the couch, closed her eyes, and was gone. As he says himself.

"I suppose it's a grand way to go. But it would have been nice to hold her hand as she slipped away. I couldn't believe the suddenness of that moment. In the blink of an eye she was gone."

He arrives at my table, coffee and biscuit cake in hand.

"Hello Jack, sit down and take the weight off your legs. How are you keeping?"

"Sure Mick I'm hanging in, trying to do the best I can with what I have left."

"Go away out of that Jack, there's many a twenty year old would give a lot to be as healthy looking as yourself, you're like a two year old. Isn't it a grand day out? We're very fortunate with the weather so far this month. I know its July and this is what we should expect at this time of year. But Jack! You know as well as I do, we've had many a bad July in the past."

"Indeed we have Mick, but let us praise the bridge as we cross it."

"Come here Jack, have you heard about Bertie O'Shea? I hear he's been shifted to the Regional yesterday evening. I believe it's his prostrate gland is giving some trouble again, the poor misfortune."

"Ah Mick sure that doesn't surprise me a bit, he's complaining about his prostrate with the last couple of years. He's a stubborn man is Bertie, he wouldn't listen to doctor, wife, or family, and anyway I think he is too embarrassed to discuss his situation with anybody. I hope he hasn't let it go too late. It's a complaint that if it's not looked after fairly quickly could be fatal and he's suffering a lot with a few years. As I say Mick I hope things work out O.K. for him. It seems the pain is almost unbearable. When you get the call of nature you've got to go straight away. The only trouble is that when you hit the toilet you cannot urinate, and the pain is excruciating. I do feel real sorry for him. We're very lucky Mick you and I."

"He's not what you'd call an old man Jack he's only 62. That's 6 years younger than either one of us. I don't think early retirement suited Bertie at all. I would say he hadn't the temperament to enjoy his idle time. Not like us Jack sure we're well able to while away the time. Jack what do you think, apart from going down six feet, is the bottom line when we depart this earth?"

"Never a dull moment with you, always asking dopey questions about some subject that others aren't a bit comfortable with. I would say for you, it would be total exclusion from any fraternising with others, until you have learned not to be making other people uncomfortable."

"Jack all I wanted was a simple answer to what I would consider a simple question."

"Mick nothing is ever simple with you, nothing is ever quite black and white. After Mass last Saturday evening I heard you asking the priest are there animals in heaven. Now why would a man like you, who never even owned a canary, want to know that? You put poor Fr., Hennessy in a very uncomfortable position, with everyone within earshot suddenly looking in his direction."

"How could I have put him in an uncomfortable position? It was a very simple question, with just one of two answers, yes or no."

"Mick you know Fr. Hennessy as long as I do. Didn't you see his left temple twitching as if it were going to burst? You also know when Fr.Hennessy is up against it his left temple starts dancing in his head and he gets rather frustrated."

"O.K! O.K! Jack, maybe it was the wrong time to ask him, but sure you'd think that it was a question a man of his calling could have answered. The way he turned on his heel and shot back into the Sacristy everyone there knew that he hadn't a clue. I wonder if he'll have the answer next Saturday."

"Mick" Jack then says to me, a bit narky I thought. "Not alone will he not have the answer he'll be avoiding you like the plague for the next couple of weeks. And who could blame him. The week before you asked that guy from the Historical and Archaeological Society, who, just happened at that time to be talking to Fr. Hennessy,

'If all fairies were Godmothers, or were some of them Godfathers?'

"It's only an oddball like you would think of something like that. They both moved away so quickly, you couldn't see their heels for the dust. That man thought you were some kind of weirdo. It's only myself could put up with you. Poor Fr. Hennessy, and him such a quiet oul' angashur. He really hasn't a clue what to make of you. You and your dopey questions."

"Jack you forget that the man with Fr. Hennessy that evening is one of those people who excavate around Fairy Forts, so why wouldn't he be the one to ask."

"Forget it Mick, come on you pest and we'll hop on the bus as far as the Lough Bar and have a quart before the lunch. It might soften you up a bit. You're as bad as the inquisition crowd of long ago."

"You know Jack maybe some other day I'll broach the subject of Heaven, Hell, Reincarnation, and animals in Heaven with Fr. Hennessy. Also what would he think of our situation today if Mary had had a baby girl? Also while I was sitting here on my own awhile ago I got to thinking,

'Did Santa and Mrs Santa have any children of their own?
Or better still, you know what? We'll see who's in the Lough Bar, and I might chance a few while we're having our couple of pints. After all some of those guys up there think their the cats whiskers, barrels of knowledge, and no subject is beyond them. Let's go."

Working Mother

'That cursed clock, I could do with another hour or two. I had better get up, Mick will be in from night work soon and if I'm still in bed he'll want to have his way before breakfast. But there's time and place for everything. I'd like a bit of lovin' just now myself, however the children must come first. By the time I'll have those three kids dressed, fed, their lunches packed, and out to school he'll be gone to bed. And all he has to do is snore his way through the day until 4.oo or 5.oo o' clock. I wish he could give up that job. I hate the shift work.'

"Come on you lot up there, time to get up your Dad will be in from work shortly and will be looking for his breakfast. So let's get the show on the road."

Still in her dressing gown Mary O'Rourke heads for the Kitchen while the kids are heard making a rush for the bathroom. Michael the eldest gets there first and bangs shut the door. The other two Sheila and Róisín, stand out side shouting,

"Hurry on Michael we're dropping"

Michael gleefully shouts back,

"I won't be long, only about a quarter of an hour. Ha! Ha! Ha!"

Róisín is heard to shout back, "Michael please don't be so mean, hurry up, the two of us are really dropping."

From the bottom of the stairs Mary's voice rises "Michael I don't want to have to go up there, but if I do, I guarantee you'll regret it."

When Michael, smiling broadly, eventually comes from the bathroom the two girls burst in. Then there's a squabble over who's going to use the toilet first. When the morning bathroom episode is over and the three have eventually got dressed and are sitting to their breakfast Mary then goes to get ready. She gets dressed quickly and just as she slips out of her slippers into her shoes, in walks Mick.

"Good morning lads, and a very nice morning it is Thank God. All ready to go? "

"Good morning Dad."

He gives Mary a kiss on the cheek, and says,

"Good morning love," And handing her €20.oo he says,

"Mary the car's a bit low on petrol so you might stop at Clancy's and put in a couple of gallons, this will keep us going for a few days. That cursed petrol is getting dearer by the hour."

"There had better be enough to get me to work after dropping the kids, as I don't have the time to get it first. Your breakfast is in the oven, I'll see you this evening love. 'Byeee" and bundles the children out the door into the car and heads for the school about, with a bit of luck, 15 minutes away. After dropping the girls first and a little further down the road Michael, she glances at the fuel gauge and decides there's enough petrol to get her to the filling station after work. She then drives to the local supermarket where she works five days a week from 9.ooam to 2.3opm. It may not be the best job in the world but the hours suit her and of course the money from it is a great help to keep the wolf from the door.

During her daily routine Mary meets almost everyone in her locality, and hears all the local gossip. Whose teenage daughter is pregnant, who's having an affair and with whom, underage drinking, who's been caught drink driving, etc., etc., etc. Even though the most of this talk is really of no interest to her she still has to listen. A number of the male customers who seem to always come to her checkout give her a bit of a lift, as they flirt with her, and tell her how smart and fresh she's looking this morning. There's one who, each time he comes to her till, passes more or less the same comment, and always calls her by her first name,

"Mary you married too young, I can't believe you're the mother of three children. That husband of yours sure is a lucky guy."

She smiles and thanks him for the compliment, at the same time he knows he hasn't a hope in hell of ever making any more progress. At any rate he's not her type, she feels he's just too good to be wholesome. A Romeo well past his sell by date. But at the same time a remark like this one always gives her a bit of a lift, and raises her morale some.

A number of those mothers she serves at the checkout she envies. Not having to work like her to make ends meet they have plenty of time to chat and gossip. Some are full of airs and graces and speak with what one might describe as a West Briton accent, not really getting the tone quite right to be convincing. But, most are nice and chatty, and enquire about the kids, how they're getting on at school and if she has anyone this year for communion or confirmation. The ones she envies are those, who, when they have their shopping done, go to the nearby café to have their morning coffee. Here they chat and take it easy for half an hour or more and on arriving home can relax with some woman's magazine; watch a nice programme such as Oprah Winfrey, the "Afternoon Show" or maybe a repeat of some soap. Also they have a cleaning lady to do all the house chores, at least when they're gone from her queue Mary doesn't have to see them again until at the soonest the next morning. She thinks of the poor cleaning lady who has to put up with them for most of the day.

With three school going kids, a mortgage, and other payments Mary cannot afford the luxury of browsing or gossiping any morning. She's got to keep her nose to the grind stone and keep smiling. Even though that morning Sheila was a bit off form and looked to be going down with the 'flu, and hopefully not anything worse, Mary still had to be at her till at

9.ooam. There's this to it of course, that those women may not have as happy a marriage as hers.

At noon she has her lunch break and then back to the till until 2,3opm.

9.30 to 10.15 and 12.30 to 1.15 are the very busy times as usually the workmen from the local building sites come to pick up something from the deli. Mary does enjoy these times; the banter between the men is sometimes very funny as they slag off one another about something, imaginary or real, that has happened on the site or maybe the night before while having a few drinks together. And most will say something like;

"Good morning Mary you're looking very well this morning."

She is happy when her stopping time eventually comes around, and it's Friday, which means she's off for the next two days. A lot of that time will be taken up washing, ironing, and other household jobs that have backed up all week.

Before leaving she picks up a few groceries and the evening paper for Mick. On her way to the school she calls to Clancy's for petrol, and arrives at the school for the children at 3.oo o'clock. Sheila is in good form and looks to have put what ever it was upset her in the morning over her. They arrive home around 3.3o and while the kids get stuck in their homework, Mary starts to get the dinner ready. No sound from upstairs Thank God. One hour later with everything under control Mary sits for awhile, picks up the evening paper and settles herself comfortably in the chair, to relax for a half hour.

But no such luck, just as she opens the page with the deaths she hears the movement upstairs. Ten minutes later Mick arrives down, looks for the paper, goes into the living room, turns on the tele, and settles down in the arm chair to read. Five minutes later he's snoring his head off as if he hadn't been in bed for a month. When he's on nights it's nearly always like this.

Mary wishes she could have a little nap just now, but with the racket Mick is making there is no hope of this. Michael gets up from his homework shakes his dad, and says,

"Dad could you please stop that awful snoring, we're trying to get our homework done and we don't have a chance with all the noise you're making."

"Look son I don't know what you're talking about, I'm sitting here quietly reading the paper, so how could I be upsetting you."

Michael retorts.

"Dad you're making the most awful racket because you're just snoring your head off. You're like a big old fat sow; the three of us are having a tough time trying to concentrate."

"O.K., I'm sorry about that lads, I'll go out to the kitchen and talk to your mam. I'll have a sconce at the paper after dinner."

He gives Mary a pat on the bum and says,

"I suppose there's no hope of going upstairs for half an hour?"

"You know Mick" she smiles "just now there is nothing I'd like better, but you know as well as I, it's utterly impossible, so sit down like a good boy and read your paper."

After dinner, around 7.oo O'clock Mick kisses Mary and the children and says, "Be good now for your Mam and I'll see you in the morning."
He then heads for the factory where he works. Even though this is only a twenty minute drive he always leaves early, as the traffic can be heavy at times.

9.3o pm the wash up finished, the kids in bed, although not yet asleep, her day has finally come to an end. Mary settles down to watch the "Late Late Show." It's been a long day and at last she can relax and look forward to a lie in tomorrow morning, with hopefully, a bit of loving thrown in as a bonus.

To whet your appetite

This morning as I drive my coach out from Galway City, and head for Connamara, with 42 American visitors on board, and, blotting out the drone of the tour guides voice, I think of all the people who have never seen this beautiful part of Ireland. Most people I know, and that includes myself, opt for a foreign holiday. We can speak at length on the wonders and beauty of places like New York, Paris, Rome, Venice and places even more exotic and further afield. Yet! What do we know about Ireland, its wonders, and its, "Forty Shades of green."

I will try to whet your appetite, to ignite a little flame of longing in you to visit this region of the West of Ireland, and to soak up its unique atmosphere. It is just a coach drivers' overview of the area known as Connamara.

Leaving the city we drive out along the coast of Galway Bay where the Atlantic gently laps its shore. This part of Galway, known as Salthill, is one of the most popular seaside areas in the country. At this particular point there aren't great sandy beaches, but it is very safe for swimming. This morning there are plenty of people walking or jogging on the promenade getting their daily dose of exercise and fresh air. On the far side of the bay we get a glimpse of the Burren of County Clare, that magnificent lunar like landscape of 100sq miles of layered limestone rock.

Approaching the village of Spiddal we get a fine view of the Aran Islands, sitting out there in the Atlantic defying sea and storm to obliterate them. Spiddal is one of the string of villages located along the shore of Galway bay. On the approach to Spiddal is a must visit to that beautiful and well laid out gift store, Standúns. Standúns specialises in top quality Irish goods at very competitive prices, and its customer service is second to none. They will also ship your purchases to any part of the world.

Spiddal gets its name from the Gaelic word for hospital, Óspidéal. Near here, believe it or not, in the19th century a hospital that catered for Lepers was founded, and each Sunday these were driven in to the church of St. Nicholas in Galway City for Sunday Service. To this day one may still see in this church the special place known as the 'Lepers Gallery.'

Travelling up the main street of Spiddal we arrive at the church of St. Enda. This church was completed in 1904, and is of modern Celtic Romanesque Architecture. It is true in every detail to the old Celtic tradition, even to the interlaced ironwork hinges on the main doors.

Walking along the footpath in Spiddal, chatting, and obviously enjoying the whole experience, is a large group of teenagers. These are pupils from some of our city schools who have come here to enjoy a few weeks' holidays, and, at the same time brushing up on their native language. All this area is known as "An Gaeltacht," where, although everyone has English, their first language would be Gaelic.

Not too far from here and about 300 metres in from the main road is a little beach known as "Trá na Bpáistí" which means the "Beach of the Babies." At one time in Ireland still born babies, or those babies that died shortly after birth and were not baptised, could not be buried in consecrated ground. It was believed that having died in the state of original sin their souls could not enter Heaven, and they went to a place called Limbo. The babies were buried in places like the sandy soil between the foreshore and the sea, or under the stone walls dividing property. These places were considered to be 'No Mans Land." Locals tell us that on 'Trá na Bpáistí' a baby is buried under every stone. Those people who committed suicide were also denied burial in consecrated ground, and found their last resting place in 'No Mans Land.'

Being a bit more enlightened today this is no longer common practise. A lone stone cross marks this very tragic and lonely place.

After passing the very modern complex and huge mast of the T.V. station "Telefis na Gaelige" or "TG4" we come to a cross roads. If one were to take the road on straight it will lead you to the little harbour of Rossaveel, and from here one can board a ferry and take a trip to the Aran Islands. Many take this trip to get away from the rat race and chill out for a few days in the peace and quietness on one of the islands. We keep to the main road and pass over a narrow bridge that brings us to the village of Cashla. Here we leave the Bay Road and turn right on to the Lake Road. In this part of County Galway, though the land is mostly flat, it is rough and scrubby. It is dotted here and there with lovely streams tumbling over rocky beds to form little waterfalls that eventually flow into one of the many small lakes, before it eventually makes its way to the sea. Though at first glance this countryside looks barren and deserted, however on closer observation one is amazed at the number of swans and other waterfowl that inhabit these lakes. On the side of some these lakes small huts, called blinds are erected. These huts are used by Ornithologists, mostly in the wintertime, when Canadian Geese, Whooper Swans, and other birds from the frozen north come here to winter. Of course foxes, rabbits, hares, stoats, and a host of other small creatures abound here. Here also if one is lucky, you may catch a glimpse of a little herd of Connamara ponies. Although their origin is uncertain, more than likely these ponies are a cross breed between the native Irish horse and Spanish – Arab ponies. These would have been imported into Ireland from Galicia in Spain in the middle ages. These animals were once the main workhorse in and around the Connamara region and now due to their stature, beauty, and passiveness, are in great demand as children's pets all over the world.

At the next cross roads we see the signpost for the lovely village of Roundstone, and, the cottage of that well known Irish patriot Pádraigh Pearse is just a few kilometres to our left. This is well worth a visit, but today we are taking the other direction. In the distance rising majestically above the lakes and bog land are the Maam Turk Mountains, and the range known as the Twelve Bens or the Twelve Pins. Maam Turk is Gaelic for "Fiery Boar."

Crossing the main Galway to Clifden road at Maam Cross we enter the narrow road between the mountains and this road winding through bog land at the foot of these mountains will bring us to Maam Bridge. We are now in the "Quiet Man" country where the film of that name was located in the 1950s, starring that legend of many Wild West films John Wayne, and that red headed Irish beauty, Maureen O'Hara.

Turning left at Maam Bridge we head for the little village of Leenane this is situated at the head of Irelands only Fjord, Killary Harbour. This area was the location for the Noel Pearson produced film "The Field" starring Richard Harris, John Hurt, and Brenda Fricker, a tragic story of one mans love of tradition and land.

This is also known as Joyce Country. Some think it is called Joyce Country because James Joyce that great Irish writer occasionally spent some time here. Why it is called Joyce country is, that many families of that name, who originally came from Wales, settled here when Cromwell roamed the land and gave the ultimatum to the Irish people, "To Hell or to Connaught." And today, many families of that name populate this region.

It is an outstandingly beautiful area of mountains, small fields, stone walls, rivers, waterfalls, and lakes. It is an area of bogs and scrubland, where sheep graze along the roadside. Only the hardy mountain sheep could find anything to eat here. There is very little cultivation here except for forestry, as most of the land is not suitable for the growing of root or grain crops. Here one can still see the farmers and cottiers cutting the peat from the bogs by the old method, using a spade like tool called a Slán, pronounced slawn. The peat, or turf as it is called locally, is cut in oblong squares of about 12inches by 4 or 5 inches and laid out in rows to dry. When it is fairly dry, it is then lifted by hand and put in what is known as stools. These are pyramid shaped, and would contain 12 or 13 sods each placed in such a manner that the wind would blow through them, and help to dry them out. After a couple of weeks like this, depending on the weather, the peat will then be brought to the roadside, ready to be taken into the vicinity of the cottage or farmhouse and stored. This is the main fuel used for heating and cooking.

Connamara derives its name from the son of an ancient Irish Chieftain named Con, who was a great warrior. The name Con means warrior, Na means of, and Mara is Gaelic for sea. This chieftains son was called Connamara, and when translated from Gaelic means, "Warrior of the Sea."

I have toured Connamara many times and still each trip holds something different, something new. It is a mythical and mystical land with ever changing moods. One minute it is dark and sultry the next minute the sun will burst through, and you joyously watch, as the clouds flit lazily across the landscape in ever changing patterns. Like someone shaking a giant patchwork quilt.

When the mist creeps eerily down from the mountains top to fill the valley below with a soft cottony blanket, this place takes on a contour all its own. One can readily believe that Leprechauns, Fairies, Puckas, Pishógs, and Poteen makers distilling their illegal and highly potent brew are all complimenting each other, and vying for a place in the onlookers' imagination.

It is a place though full of grandeur, still holds the signs of poverty and famine which scourged our country in the 1840s and '50s. Evidence of this can be plainly seen in the remains of the Lazy beds that scar the hillsides around Leenane. These beds are where the peasants planted their potatoes prior to, and up to, the great famine. The remains' of these lazy beds are a stark epitaph of a people discarded and left to die.

Their history is our history.

On we travel from Leenane, skirting around the shore of Irelands only fjiord, Killary Harbour. Opposite on the other side of the Fjiord are the Mweelree Mountains of county Mayo. Killary harbour is the divide between the counties of Galway and Mayo. Next we come to Kylemore Abbey. Kylemore Abbey, a magnificent late 19th century limestone and granite castellated building erected by a British merchant named Mitchell Henry, as a present to his wife. It is now the home of an order of Benedictine nuns, and one of our top boarding schools for girls. Nestling against its mountainous backdrop, it is indeed in a unique and spectacular setting. The lake on which the abbey is situated is named "Loch an Coille Mór," the "Lake of the big wood". Kylemore is the Anglicisation of Coille Mór. One should linger here a little while. Visit the abbey, the gardens, the gift shop, and partake of a nice leisurely lunch in its beautiful spacious restaurant.

Leaving Kylemore we turn left and a short distance from here we turn right and take the road across the Inagh Valley. This valley road runs between the Twelve Bens to link up with the main Clifden to Galway road again. The valley with its lakes, mountains, and forestry, with its quick change of light and shadow defies description. Even with brush or camera one could never hope to capture its true beauty.

As we reach the main road we turn left for Galway. A few kilometres to our right is Ballinahinch Castle, this was once one of the strongholds of the Pirate Queen Grace O'Malley. Later it was owned by an M.P. called Richard Martin who introduced the bill in Westminster that lead to the founding the Royal Society for the Prevention of Cruelty to Animals. This earned him the nick name "Humanity Dick."

Travelling the main road towards Galway we pass through the towns of Oughterard, whose name means "The high Meadow" and Moycullen meaning "The valley of the Holly." In Moycullen one may linger awhile at the Connamara Marble factory. This is a family owned business, and Mr. Ambrose Joyce Senior, or Junior, will be only too delighted to give you a tour of the factory. You will be shown the Connamara Marble being cut, polished, and crafted into all types of souvenirs and jewellery, fit to adorn any lady's finery. Also in Moycullen a visit to Celtic Crystal to watch the blowers and engravers at work is well worth the stop, and you will marvel at their skill when you view the finished product. Celtic Crystal specialises in multi-coloured vases and other crystal products. For a unique once off piece, just give them a rough sketch, and they will be only too happy to oblige.

Driving on towards Galway we travel down the western shore of Lough Corrib. This beautiful lake is famous for its Salmon fishing, and fishermen come here from all over the world to test their skill against the great fish. One may also take a cruise on Lough Corrib. Starting in Galway or other points up river and finish with high tea at the magnificent Ashford Castle, on the lakes most northerly point. This is an experience to be savoured, and will be remembered and recounted long after you have finished the trip.

Back then to Galway the "City of the Tribes" also known as the Gateway to Connamara. Galway is a city for leisurely sight seeing; to walk around it is a revelation. There's the Catholic Cathedral of Our Lady assumed into heaven and St. Nicholas. St. Nicholas is the patron saint of Galway. See Lynchs Castle, where, the one time Mayor of Galway, James Lynch Fitzsimons lived, and nearby the window of the jail where he hung his only son Walter for the murder of another young man. This act of Lynchs brought the word "Lynching" into the English vocabulary. Nearby in the Bowling Green area is the home of Nora Barnacle, wife of writer James Joyce. Go and see one of the last remnants of Spanish influence at the Spanish Arch. Visit the little harbour near the legendary Claddagh area, where legend says Columbus came ashore to attend Service in the church of St.Nicholas, before continuing his voyage to the New World. A little limestone sculpture at this spot commemorates this event.

Walk around Eyre square and view the statue erected to Pádraigh O'Connaire one of our most loved Gaelic writers. Here also is a very striking memorial to the Galway Hooker. The Galway Hooker was a little sailing craft that at one time sailed with provisions between the mainland and the Aran Islands. Dominating the upper side of Eyre Square is the Browne Door, another piece of Spanish architecture.

Galway is a vibrant city, full of Buskers and other street entertainers, and thanks to its fine university, a city of young people. It has some very fine hotels, guest houses and hostels, is renowned for its horse racing, art and music festivals, and it is quite an experience to shop in its narrow winding streets. Galway has such a variety of eating places, from gourmet to the traditional fish and chips, that all palates and pockets are well catered for. There is a lot more I could say about Galway and Connamara. About its world famous ponies, the Rhododendron and Fuchsia that grow profusely all over this county, Wild Iris, Bog Oak or the amount and variety of ancient artefacts that have been found in the bogs there. But as I said at the beginning, this is a coach drivers' overview of Connamara and Galway and it's just "To whet your appetite."

A visit to this area of the Emerald Isle could be the ultimate experience of ones holiday.

Freedom of Speech

Have you ever stopped to think about "Freedom of Speech?" This is a phrase that is bandied around a lot at the moment. It is a phrase that has lost a lot of its meaning because of the way it is interpreted. It is used by some, who feel they have the right to express their opinion no matter what to insult or hurt others. It is also used in certain areas such as Parliament, scathingly, so that one may utter something untrue, and, knowing it to be untrue still says what he or she has to, just to try and score some points over their opposite number. Thanks to privilege of Parliament, the injured party may not be able to instigate proceedings against the one who uses "Freedom of Speech" in this manner. Or, what use would "Freedom of Speech" be if the people we're addressing, are totally deaf and dumb, and could not relate verbally or otherwise their feelings about what you have said in the last 5 to 7 minutes.

The voice is truly a unique organ and as such should be treasured and cared for and never abused. Without voice it must be very hard to express ones emotions fully and satisfactorily. I'm sure it must be very stressful, and at times, can leave one with a terrible feeling of aloneness and hopelessness.

As members of Toastmasters International we are indeed privileged people to be able to use our voices to entertain, debate, or even educate our fellow members. We are encouraged by our organisation to get up there and tell it like it is, and maybe sometimes tell it like it isn't. In this we should really count our blessings.

I wonder, if a person who is deaf and dumb may become a member of Toastmasters, have we the facilities to facilitate such a person? Or is it something not very feasible, that provisions could be made to accommodate someone in this position? I can only speak for myself, as I would be considered one who is what we might call, 'hard of hearing.'

I love Toastmasters I sit at meetings and do my best to follow what is happening around me. I can tell you some times I fail miserably.

In Toastmasters you have people from all walks of life, therefore you are bound to have people with different pitches of voice, and so while some are quite audible, others speak at a very low pitch and cannot be heard by hard of hearing people like me. It can also be rather embarrassing for one at Topic Sessions when one must ask the Topics master more often than not to repeat the topic. You try to overcome this by making a funny remark about your loss of hearing. I am very thankful that I do have the use of my voice, and so may ask for a repeat of the topic. Some can understand your frustration of not being able to hear first time, and pity you. Well, the last thing you want is pity, what you want is a little more understanding and patience from others in the room. Just think about it!

Probably to a certain extent if a microphone could be used it would be a big help to a hard of hearing person.

Then, what about the person who is deaf and dumb? His or hers only mode of communication is through sign language. Either everyone in the room can read sign language, or, an interpreter must be used. For them it must be terribly frustrating as they wonder if their interpreter, although highly professional, is giving the right emphasis to their speech.

How then can a person with these disabilities, project themselves and with sign language put proper emphasis on a point which is tantamount to their speech? It must indeed be very hard and take a lot of practice. Is there anyway that Toastmasters can cater for this person? I'm only asking the question, I don't have any solution. It is a dilemma for Toastmasters, but one that with a bit of thought may not be so hard to overcome. As I've already said I don't have the answer. I would think that some kind of communication education programme may be the answer. Wouldn't it be wonderful to breach this communication blockage, to welcome those with this disability and bring a new dimension to Toastmasters?

I once met a man who is totally blind and had the use of a guide dog. It was amazing how this man put so much confidence in his dog to guide him through crowds, traffic around the city, and up the isle of the church on Sundays to his proper seat. This man would also go daily to the City Library and read the papers, and so could keep up with the news of the day at home and abroad. He was able to do this because he was fully conversant in Braille, and very lucky that the library was able to accommodate him. Being a very apt reader in Braille he also had read quite a number of the Classics which had been translated into this form of writing.

At one time we spoke of his disability and I asked if he considered blindness a bigger disability than deafness. He laughed and said to me,

"You know Pat, blindness may be considered a major setback in life, but, it is one that with a little faith, courage, and of course a good dog can be overcome to a certain degree. Now deafness is another kettle of fish altogether. Deafness, unless one is very efficient in lip reading, one is completely excluded from ordinary everyday conversation. A deaf person is always on the periphery, and hardly ever part of the crowd."

Another thing he said is, "If I could not listen to my music I may as well be dead."

So again I say "Think about it! Everyone may not be gifted like we are, with what we call "Freedom of Speech." And now Toastmasters I leave you with this thought. As I said earlier, do not abuse, but take care, and respect the wonderful faculties you have been bestowed with.

In Hindsight

After achieving so much, and after collecting many awards in the literary world, Marcus McPherson was not a happy man. Tonight, his contempories in the literary world, friends, others involved in the commercial side of the city, and some of his one time students from university. All had come together to celebrate his 70th birthday and his formal retirement from his position of "Professor of Literature" at the University. A position he had held for 30 years.

Outside, he looked very calm and collected. Inside, the torment of years lost lay heavily on his mind. Each one as they arrived clasped his hand, congratulated him, and thanked him for the knowledge he had so liberally imparted on them. All wished him a long and happy retirement. He looked around the room, no family to be seen, although each had been sent an invitation. It would have meant the world to him if they had turned up.

Tonight he was been wined, dined, and fêted by his peers. Congratulations came hot and heavy from all, on the many achievements of his long career in education. Some had spoken glowingly of him, and many anecdotes were told by those who thought they knew him intimately. None had a bad word to say. A reporter and photographer from the local and a national paper were also in attendance. Yet, inside Marcus was far from happy and found no matter how hard he tried, he could not give his full concentration to the night that was in it.

Pondering, not on the gains, but on the losses and heartbreak unknown to most of those around him, that life had thrown at him. Now in the midst of all this camaraderie, he could see that most of his misfortune had been of his own making. The love of his job and his thirst for work made him the epitome of a workaholic, and so his home and family had suffered.

He had longed to show his wife Sally, who came from Glengarriffe in West Cork, the hills and glens of his native Scotland. Somehow it had never come to pass. There was always a Lecture, a Seminar, a Conference, along with his usual classes, where his attendance was requested. Unfortunately he could never say "No." So a trip to his beautiful Scotland with Sally and their two sons never materialised.

The sons had married and doing very well in the legal world. Their wives were also professional people. Neither had yet started a family, and to become a grandparent Marcus would now give up every academic honour he had achieved during his lifetime. Five years ago Sally had packed her bags and left a short note on the kitchen table. The note stated that she had enough of being second best to his career and went back to west Cork. Thirty years of marriage to him and many major disappointments had culminated in a nervous breakdown, and the depression she now suffered periodically had got to her. She had spent six months in hospital and didn't intend to spend any more time wasting away in some institution or other, as would be bound to happen if she stayed with him. She was now taking a new look at her life and hopefully would, even at this late stage, find some meaning to it. She felt she would not be lonely in West Cork as many of her old friends were still living around her home place.

The boys at this stage are all set up and going their own way and didn't need her anymore, so she would return to her roots. When she was settled in she would come with the local carrier and collect her personal stuff, and that would be the end of her contact with him.

When her mother had died, Sally, being an only child, was left the cottage, and whatever furniture and other bits and pieces her mother had gathered over the years. It had a nice garden front and rear, which at this stage was well overgrown, but given time it wouldn't be all that hard to bring it back to life again. Its location overlooking Bantry bay made it indeed a prime piece of property. Over the years Sally had been tempted to sell the place. Big money had been offered for it, now she was very glad she had held on to it. She would be happy here for the rest of her days.

Marcus never went to West Cork to meet her at her home. He had written many letters asking her, no, begging her to come back to him, and never again would anyone or anything come between them. This was a promise made with his right hand on the Holy Bible. If only she would come back and try again he was sure things would be so much better. Sally wrote only once, and made it very clear that she had no intention of ever going back to him. And she kept that promise. If he wanted to start divorce proceedings, a legal separation, or leave things as they are, this would be alright with her. The choice would be his. The day before she arrived for her belongings she phoned and told him she would be up next day for her stuff. She gave him the approximate time of her arrival and asked that he would not be there at that time. When finished she would put the house key through the letter box.

He had kept away from the house on that day, and left her on her own to take whatever she had wanted from the house. On arriving back in the evening he looked around, and now that her belongings were gone, it didn't resemble at all the house he had left that morning. Most of the furniture was still there. It was the little things; photographs, bric-a-brac, and the personal stuff that Sally reckoned were hers. It wasn't a whole lot in the end, but the memories that went with these items were huge. The boys Graduation certificates, their weddings, and other photographs of the different stages of their lives. These were, up to then, all small and seemingly insignificant objects that had adorned the walls over the years. Now that they were gone, the walls on which they had hung were obvious and stark in their nakedness, and their removal, for Marcus, had broken the chain of continuity.

When their mother was around the boys and their wives were regular visitors. When Sally left they had rarely came to see him, but had at least paid a fortnightly visit their mother. Their feelings were that Marcus was the sole reason for the breakup of the family, and Marcus would be the first to acknowledge this.

With all he had achieved in academia, it now amounted to nothing. After tonight he would just be another lonely old man trying to come to terms with the past and wondering where it all went wrong. He had every material comfort, but, without Sally and the love of his boys he had nothing to heighten his spirit.

Now driving home in the evening with all the praise and the back slapping finished, a vacuum settled in. A cloud of despair came to rest over Marcus. As he drove home to his empty house, the realisation hit, that from now on he would be completely alone, he wouldn't even have his work. All his life he had been an avid book collector and he supposed he had a lot of reading to catch up on. He didn't think this would suffice and keep him occupied for long, and if he lived for another twenty years he still wouldn't have read them all. Feeling quite low now, with one quick turn of the steering wheel he turned the car and headed towards the river, after this night of glory would come, oblivion. Whatever made him waver for a split second he had no explanation, something at the last instant did and he swerved from the quayside back on to the road. Stopping the car for a minute, the thought came to him, 'Whatever about anything else the boys and Sally would never forgive him for ending his life like this'

He buried his head in his hands over the steering wheel and cried pitifully. Was there something could be salvaged from this mess even now? Damn it! It was not going to end like this. Why should it? There was too much unfinished business. Tomorrow is another day, the first day of the rest of his life, and he would as they say 'Take the bull by the horns' and try and straighten things out once and for all. It may take more than one visit to West Cork, but who cares; he had plenty of time from now on.

He still loved Sally very much, and once again his heart ached for the companionship of his sons. Maybe after all this time something can be salvaged, and the emptiness of those loveless years forgotten, left in the past. If he had won her heart all those long years ago, he might with a little faith, hope, and a lot of luck, do so again. Even the smallest glimmer of hope was better than the hollowness of his life just now.

No more phone calls, tomorrow he would drive to West Cork. In hindsight it's just possible that Sally too after five years had enough of isolation, but, if she still wanted to live in West Cork, he would gladly up his roots in the city, and if she could see her way to take him back they would end their days together. And then who knows, "Roll on the Grandchildren."

A walk with my dog

As a slight wind blows, a drop of rain hits my head,
Leaves fall lazily from the trees,
I'm well wrapped up,
So Jack Frost nipping at my nose is no problem.
I look to my right; the sun shines over Shandon,
On top its Goldy Fish glistens,
To my left, from a little dark cloud a few drops of rain,
I think to myself 'typical Irish weather.'
This does not take from the beauty of this morning,
My dog Jack with a skip in his step walks happily
alongside,
Can he understand that there's something special
About this day, and about this time of the year.
For today is the 1st of December,
And in 24 days time it will be Christmas.
I am still at the 1st and for now that's where I will stay.
And I look again at the Goldy Fish glistening over
Shandon,
I thank God for this beautiful, beautiful day.

Graham Cooney, age 12.

Legion of Mary

In 1947 at thirteen years of age I joined St. Finbarrs Boys Club on Copley Street. It was for boys from age 14 to 18, but somehow I was accepted and spent five happy years there as a member. An old grandaunt of mine who would be scolded for putting three pence out of her pension each week into the Boys Club Box on the counter of the Post Office on Douglas Street, would always point to me and say;
"Someday he'll reap the harvest of that widow's mite."
My God how right she was.
The building was originally the home of Redmond's Hurling and Football Club who moved from here to the basement of the Carpenters Hall on Fr. Matthew Quay. After awhile they moved to bigger and better premises on Tower Street, which they renovated, and this is still their home.
It consisted of two rooms, with a full sized snooker or billiard table down stairs, and a much larger room upstairs. In the upstairs room, which was dominated by a fairly large statue of the Blessed Virgin with a little blue light flickering at its base, we played table tennis, snooker on a smaller table than the one downstairs, darts, rings, draughts and other board games. A Quiz, be it on spelling or on general knowledge, was always very popular especially in winter time, when we all would gather round a blazing fire and one of the brothers would be the Quiz Master. In one corner of this room was a piano which a few learned to play, or should I say, knocked a tune or two out of. We also had a drama class, run by two very dedicated members Dave Twomey and Tom Madden, with the help of Mick Barry, who tried to make us all pioneers. He did succeed with a few. This drama group won the "Jack Lynch Perpetual Trophy" three years in a row. Who can forget Paddy Martin? Paddy a gifted handyman, made

all the stage sets for the dramas in his spare time. He worked delivering coal for Tedcastles which was not an easy job as one can imagine, humping bags of coal up flights of stairs in the old tenements was no easy task. Paddy was also our table tennis coach but always found time, mostly after the club closed for the night at 10.30 pm, to make those sets. He was certainly gifted at this work.

What I do remember with fondness is the selflessness and the time given voluntarily by members of the South Parish Legion of Mary Presidium, "Refuge of Sinners" who met in the Legion rooms on Mary Street each Monday night from 7.30pm to 9.00pm. While the brothers were attending their meeting some people from U.C.C. would open up and supervise us until the regular men came.

These men manned the club seven nights a week, and for the five the years I was a member I cannot recall it being closed one night for lack of supervisory personnel.

In the long summer evenings, weather permitting, the brothers, you may not be aware of this, but all senior male legionaries are called brother, would walk us youngsters to Pouladuff where a field was made available to the club and there we played football, hurling and other field and track sports. Actually St. Finbarrs Boys club was the cradle of the very successful St. Finbarrs Athletic Club. I believe the Jack Lynch trophy won by the drama group in those far off days is still competed for yearly by members of the Athletic club. Two of its founder members were John O'Connell from Evergreen Street and Dickie Day from Nicholas Hill. Other staunch legionaries from Nicholas Hill were the brothers Bobby and Owen McCarthy, Mick Barry, Joe Holt, Ernie Lake. Owen McCarthy also made his mark as a fine soccer referee.

At 8.45pm each evening we all gathered around the statue of our Blessed Mother and recited the rosary.

There were other boys clubs in the city too. There were Fr.O'Learys on the Bandon Road, St. Peter and Paul's, on French Church Street, off Patrick Street, Fr.O'Learys, Shandon Street, and the News Boys Club situated near the Opera House. The competiveness in snooker, table tennis, and field sports between clubs was indeed very keen. We certainly had no problems with clubs from other denominations either. I remember going to the Synagogue on the South Terrace to play in a table tennis tournament, and the Jewish lads who were at that time involved in inter club competition came to play in our club on many occasions. When it came to rosary time on the night we hosted the games they went to the snooker room down stairs, and when the rosary was finished came back up to resume the competition. You might say we practised ecumenism before the word was even invented. At the time I never heard anyone wonder or question why we should be involved with other religions.

Today our clubs are so different. We have mixed youth clubs run on a business like format by fully professional people who have graduated in Psychology, Social Science or from other community courses.

The Legion of Mary brothers, who looked after us young boys and gave freely of their time and experience, were certainly a credit to that organisation. They always treated us with a caring love and respect. There wasn't any government grant or monies available from other sources. The only income was from the box on the local Post Office counter, or maybe a few shillings from the secret bag which was handed around at the weekly Legion meetings. For the members the weekly script was four pennies, but if some week your parents were unable to afford this it didn't matter, no one, only the brother on charge on script night knew this, and he would never reveal it to another soul. These were hard times, money was scarce, and those men understood this.

Another thing on their agenda was, if a boy was missing for four or five nights two of the brothers would call to his home and enquire if everything was O.K., They were always on the alert in case a boy might be using the club as an excuse to their parents and then going else where. This was a very good system and was much appreciated by the parents.

I am now looking back over 60 years and cannot recall all their names. Other brothers I remember with a great fondness are;

Our President Chris "Pop" Woods, Joe Meany, Paddy Martin, Tom Cooke, Michael and Noel O'Sullivan, Paul Phillips, Pearse Wise, Bill Davis, Noel Woods, and a man with a great operatic voice Richard Woods. Our Spiritual Director was Fr. Jim Cashman, who later became Parish Priest at Innishannon; he was followed by Fr. Denis O'Connor, who now I believe is a Monsignor. There were a lot more who gave unselfishly of their time and expertise, I can see them in my minds eye but unfortunately I cannot remember their names. I hope they will forgive me. Most of these men have passed on to their eternal reward, may the light of Heaven shine brightly on them today.

I will finish by saying 'Thank God' that I was associated during my growing and learning years with these wonderful gentlemen of the Legion of Mary. If the founder of the Legion Frank Duff knew these men I'm sure he would be very proud of them for continuing to pass on the ideals of this very worthy organisation.

The Gossips

Marge O'Hanlon and Hannah Cogley two old friends meet on Shandon Street. As usual local affairs and scandal, real or imagined, are discussed in the most intimate and secretive manner. When Hannah and Marjorie meet, the shopping always takes second place to some new piece of scandal that may be unfolding in the parish.

"Good morning Marge."

"Good morning Hannah."

"Beautiful morning thank God."

"It is indeed Han, and long may it last."

"Sure it's nearly time we got a bit of sunshine, is it any wonder we're all pains and aches. Most of the time this country is only fit for ducks, and sometimes it's so wet even the ducks go for shelter. Still when you look around you, I suppose we have a lot to be thankful for as well. I mean Marge did you see the news last night on the Tele? In one country there are floods so bad thousands of people have to be evacuated from their homes, and somewhere else there are forest fires raging, and there's such a shortage of water, that the whole country could be burned to a cinder. "

"True for you indeed Hannah girl, but you know isn't it fine for some of our own to be able to go gallivantin' out to them foreign places, and warm their backsides in the sun for a week or two. God when we were young if we could get the train to Youghal or the bus down to Crosshaven on Sunday, we were in Heaven. Han where do they get the money? I tell you Hannah 'twould be a lot better for their kids if they put a bit more grub on the table rather than bringing them out to those oul' foreign places. Then they're showing off their all over tan when they return home, and I mean an all over tan. Sure I believe Han they're stretched on the beaches in their birthday suit, pure naked. Not a stitch on them. You know Hannah a tan never filled an empty belly, so it didn't"

"Marge don't you know there up to their eyes in debt. Shur they borrow it from the Credit Union or some bank or other. Everything they have is on the H.P. I see Kitty Flaherty's fella has changed his car again, and she's the only wan workin' in that family. It's true for you with all that grandeur and all that swannin' around the world; they couldn't have it on the table, Marge they have to be short somewhere. God forgive them."

"Come here I want you Han, I don't know how true it is but I hear Billy Twomey is on the ran-tan again, and his poor Mary hardly cold in her grave. I wouldn't mind Hannah, but he all but threw himself into the grave after her. Everyone was talking about how he would miss her, and probably would not be long more after her. There all the same Han once you're gone you're gone and that's about the size of it."

"Go away, what do you mean by that Marge?"

"Now Han you must surely have noticed the carry on of him at the club last Sunday night. I wasn't there myself but Maggie Fennel told me he was flying his kite with that oul' jade Bridie Carey all night."

"God knows Marge, sure I'm only living two doors from him, and myself and Jamesy were in the club on Sunday night, I didn't see anything suspicious about his behaviour. Of course we weren't there very long, we just had one drink and left."

"Well from what I hear from Josey Sullivan as well, he's far from behaving like a widower in mourning. His poor departed Mary how she slaved for him and his brood. Married for 40 years and in the end it doesn't mean a thing."

"Now Marge I don't think you're quite right there. I mean Bridie Carey! She's young enough to be his daughter."

"Be that as it may Hannah, you know that wan well enough. Her motto is 'If you have it, flaunt it.' And in that mini-skirt she wears, boy is she able to flaunt it. Han, she's not that young either, I'd say she's in her late Thirty's."

"I remember Marge when she was growing up, you'd think butter wouldn't melt in her mouth. And her poor mother was telling everyone that would listen, about Bridie going to join the Poor Clare's after her leaving cert. After her leaving cert is right, she only just finished her primary when she went to work making black and white pudding in Denny's cellar. Now I'm not saying anything bad about that job, didn't me own father, God rest him, work there hanging the pigs for nearly 40 years. I'm afraid Bridies calling for the Poor Clare's went down the shore with the slurry."

"Well bless your memory Han, God knows that's the truest word you ever spoke. And if I remember correctly 'tis Lizzie herself should have joined the Poor Clare's. Wasn't she always runnin' up to the church for Novenas and rosaries and if there was Benediction within a mile of our street she'd be over there in a flash. All the candles she'd light in front of the blessed virgins altar, 'twould be like the towering inferno before she'd be finished. My God! She was a very holy woman. I'd say Lizzie, God rest her, wouldn't like to hear of that carry on by one of her daughters."

"Of course Bridie is the only one of the family who never married, and the only one left in the house now with her father. From what I hear at this stage, he's a right handful, but then, wasn't he always very cranky, sure you couldn't look sideways at him. Poor Lizzie going to the church and lighting a few candles, was the only bit of outing she got. He was as mean as ditch water, that fella was. I don't think I'd ever seen them out together."

"My God! Out together? He'd tell you they couldn't afford it on his money. He always had a few bob for a couple of pints himself though. A mangey oul' thing that's what he was, and still is. Oh! Oh! I'll have to go now Marge, look who's coming down the street that oul' Maisie Butler wan, she'd talk the ass off a pot, and she never has a good word to say about anyone."

"Maisie Butler is it? I'm off too Han. That wan, all she does is gossip. She should be ashamed of herself the way she goes around talking about others. A dirty back-biting oul' jade that's all she is. I must go into the market now for a bit of bodice for Jamesys dinner. He loves the bodice with the curly green cabbage and the Ballycotton Kerr's Pink spuds. I might see you again in the morning. In the meantime I'll keep my eyes and ears open, and I'll make a few enquiries about the carry on of that Bridie Carey wan. And Han as we say up in Beverly Hills have a nice day."

"And you too Marge, God bless girl."

Bí Ullamh!!

Friday January 11th 2008. Nice morning, nice day, and I am in pretty good form. So I think that, after lunch I'll do some work on my novel "A Final Reckoning."

Just after finishing lunch Mary says,

"That bit of a roof from the house to the out house is so dirty it's really bugging me. You might give it a rub of a brush some day you get a chance."

Not giving it another thought I say,

"Straight away"

"No, no" she said, "Some day you have a bit of time on your hands. I know you want to do some writing today."

"Look" I said "I'll do it now and finish with it, and then do the writing"

She looks at me gobsmacked, she couldn't believe her ears. I'm going to do the job straight away no procrastinating, no messing.

I go down to the garden shed get out the ladder, the sweeping brush, a small shovel and a plastic bag. The ladder being a bit wonky and the yard with a slight slope I steady it with a piece of timber under the leg on the lower side, I throw the brush and shovel up on the roof and climb the ladder on to the roof and proceed to clean the lean-to. When the job is finished I put the dirt into a plastic bag and hand it down to Mary and leave the brush and the shovel in a position near the ladder so I can reach it easily when getting down. Standing back a little from the lean-to, I admire a job well done.

I then go to get down from the roof. With one foot on the roof and the other on the ladder, the ladder slips and both of us, myself and the ladder, bite the dust. Like a sack of spuds I landed on the concrete slabs in front of the Barna.

My God! The pain, the shock, and I could hardly breathe. A stinging pain in my back and an almighty pain in my left foot told me straight away I could be in deep trouble. My foot was swelling at such a rate inside the shoe that I thought it would surely burst. Mary, who was inside the house at the time, heard the shouting and bawling and rushed out to see what all the commotion was about, when she saw my situation I believe she got as big a shock as I did. Even though she did get a fierce shock she didn't panic, she said,

"Don't move I'll be back." And ran inside the house again.

When she returned, she gently put a pillow under my head and put some blankets over me and again said,

"Don't move I'll be back." And went and phoned the ambulance.

"Don't move!" As I lay there in pure agony thoughts were flying through my mind. "Don't move! Don't move!" My God "I ask myself "am I ever going to move again?"

Johnny Curran from Toor, Waterville, Co. Kerry flashed into my head. Here was a young and very fit man who fell only about eight feet from some scaffolding around thirty years ago, and ended up a quadriplegic, paralysed from the neck down. Imagine, it happened over thirty years ago and he still can't move a muscle in the whole of his body. With the aid of a computer and some very sensitive sensors attached to his chin, he has written a very nice and indeed a sometimes very light hearted book called "Just my luck." This book tells all about the experience of himself and his family in coping with this new situation they found themselves in. It is indeed well worth a read.

Just now I mustn't even contemplate such a fate. As I'm lying there unable to move, along with the pain, and the cold, the dampness up through the concrete slabs becomes almost unbearable. On top of everything else I could die from hypothermia before the ambulance arrived. While Mary is waiting at the front door watching for the ambulance all these unpleasant thoughts are rumbling through my mind. And I pray silently but fervently,

"Lord please don't let it end like this."

After what I reckoned at the time to be about two hours, but it was really only around fifteen minutes, the ambulance crew arrive. Two paramedics and a trainee from the Navy. Thinking that at this stage as far as pain was concerned I had passed the worst. Man was I in for a shock? Unable to bring the trolley from the ambulance through the house they brought a stretcher instead. Unfortunately for me when I fell I landed too near the Barna shed and they were unable to put the stretcher down flat and roll me on to it. Then one of them asked if I could roll forward a little so they could place the stretcher under me and then roll back again.

'Oh God!' I thought 'is this guy for real? Here I am busted to bits, dying from hypothermia, and this guy asks me to roll over.' I just muttered,

"Not a hope."

Anyway between the jigs and the reels and me roaring my head off, I'm eventually lying on the stretcher. At least now I'm lying straight, and apart from the hardness of the stretcher it's not too bad. However then came the strapping down, my head was put into a kind of a plastic helmet and strapped into an immovable position. Then I was strapped across my chest, after that a strap was placed across my knees and one across my ankles. I had now become an extension of that stretcher, where it went I went I had no option. After that, came the journey out to the ambulance, it was parked in the driveway of our home. Along with our son Finbarr, a neighbour Phillip O'Leary from across the road had to be recruited to help get me and the stretcher out through the house. We, myself and the stretcher, had to be brought through the sitting room, out the hallway, half way under the stairway, down the steps at the front door, resting us for a few seconds on the garden wall, and up the steps into the ambulance. Being strapped so rigidly on the stretcher and unable to move an inch all I could see on this journey was the blue sky overhead, and thanked God it wasn't raining.

The transferring from the stretcher to the ambulance bed wasn't too painful and as I was being strapped down again in the ambulance, I thought the roughest part of the journey to the Cork University Hospital must surely be over now. Again how wrong I was. The doors banged shut and we moved out of our driveway and headed for the C.U.H. I would say in all honesty that this vehicle was one that was possibly salvaged from the Red Cross after World War 1. Air bags or even springs to cushion the humps and bumps on the journey I swear were non existent on this vehicle. Every little hump, pebble, or pothole between Churchfield and the hospital became my persecutor. These drove red hot nails into my back and foot; if it was Easter Week I thought, I might indeed be on the road to Calvary. The traffic was so heavy and moving so spasmodically, that at each lurch I felt I was been thrown around the inside of the ambulance like a shuttle cock. After a journey that I'm pretty sure Humpty Dumpty would certainly not have survived, we arrive at the Cork University Hospital.

Getting from the ambulance on to a trolley was another ordeal, not the fault of the ambulance personnel I can assure you. These were certainly pros. Looking back now I'm sure that with a broken heel and a broken bone in the back my Guardian Angel would be at the pin of his collar to get me from A to B without causing me any pain. Anyway here I am being wheeled on this trolley and landed in a corridor somewhere in the bowels of this huge hospital, wondering if I'll ever see daylight again. At this point Mary joins me.

After a little time elapsed a doctor came and asked if I wanted some pain killers, I said,

"Oh my God yes."

Would I like tablets or an injection? Not being the bravest person in the world, I opted for the tablets. Next someone started pushing the trolley from behind and a male voice said,

"You've got to go for an x ray" and pushed me along another corridor to the x ray room. On arrival I was slipped from the trolley on to the x ray table. Since I took the pain killers the pain has got worse in both my back and my foot. I tried to do all the twists and turns the girl asked me to do even though I was really hurting a lot. Then all hell broke loose, on top everything I got a cramp in my left foot. My God I really started roaring, never before in my life have I experienced the pain that I now had in my left foot. I was screaming so much that the girl eventually called for a doctor. When he came he said,

"Oh it's you is it? It's your own fault you wouldn't take the injection awhile ago."

He gave me the injection, which I found out later was morphine, I could not believe it that within half a minute the pain in my foot and back was no more. The girl was then able to take the rest of the x rays and I was deposited on my trolley out into the corridor again. At this stage I still didn't know in what part of the hospital I was. I just lay there and waited. I had heard of people being left on these trolleys for days without ever getting into a ward. I couldn't find anything wrong with the trolley itself, as far as I could see the attention and treatment one got was just the same as if one was in a ward, and it was just as comfortable, if one in my state could be made to feel comfortable, as a bed.

It was its location was the problem. The lack of privacy and the hoards of people passing up and down the corridor made you think that you were stuck somewhere between the main entrance and exit of the hospital. With all the noise no matter what ones complaint was, one had no hope whatsoever of getting any sleep. Being placed across the corridor from some open office space where phones were constantly ringing and there was a constant flow of talk I found that I was left in a really bad location. Despite the pain killers and the morphine there definitely was no hope of rest not to mind sleep. Sometime during the night a nurse came along to check blood pressure and temperature, and said she would shift me to a quieter place.

I don't know what time of the night or morning this was, but after a short time this quieter place turned out to be just as bad. It turned out to be, as far as I could make out, near the goods entrance to the hospital. The banging and the clashing of van doors and of goods being rolled in to the area and empty containers being rolled out, it was away worse than the part I had come from. Sometime during the morning I was shifted again to another corridor. This was a bit more civilised and I wondered if I was coming closer to being accommodated in a ward.

It's now Saturday 12th and still stuck in the corridor I haven't a clue what time it is. I got some breakfast and because I was flat on my back I just hadn't a hope of eating it. Then all the toing and froing, of nurses taking blood pressure and temperature and giving me pills and injections etc. Each one asking me what had happened, and none telling me what was happening. I eventually, sometime before night fall was wheeled into a ward still on my trolley. With the help of a porter and a nurse I was put in a semi sitting position and given food. I can't remember what kind it was because I was so hungry at this time I didn't care.

A Doctor came and informed me that I would be shifted to the Orthopaedic Hospital in the morning as I had a broken bone in my back and torn ligaments in my foot. This he said is what the x-rays showed. I can't remember much more about my stay in this ward. I probably got another injection and slept for awhile. Next morning Sunday morning around 11.30am I was brought by ambulance to the Orthopaedic Hospital, Gurranebraher. I believe this time it was a more modern vehicle as I found the journey quite smooth. Arriving at the hospital I was transferred from the ambulance to a bed in the male ward, with the minimum of hassle. The first thing that hit me was the quietness in this ward. There were 14 beds and only 5 were occupied. No trolleys, no hustle, no bustle, everything under control.

A nurse told me after she propped me up in the bed,

"All you have to do now Patrick is, after dinner lie down and for the rest of the time you will be with us rest your back, and no heroics please. By that, I mean no jumping out of and into the bed, you need complete rest. There will be no need for any of this as we are here to look after your every whim. In the mean time if there is anything you require just press the buzzer located at the side of your bed, and someone will come to your aid straight away.

I said,

"What about my foot? That's a lot more painful than my back."

"O.K Pat the ligaments in your foot are badly torn and this needs complete rest also."

"How long do you think I will be here for?"

"In the morning the consultant will be in to see you and he's the man who will answer all your questions. You know Patrick from what I hear you're very lucky to be alive and while you lie there you may give this some thought."

Of course she was right and I did meditate on my situation for awhile. Thinking about life, how fickle and how uncertain it can be, and when it comes down to brass tacks in one split second how every thing can change. The time between life and death can be so minuscule, so sudden, that the Boy Scouts three finger salute and motto "Bi Ullamh" this in English means "Be Ready" should never be too far from our minds, for any situation that should suddenly arise.

After a second x-ray it is found that a bone in my left heel is broken and so I'm fitted with what is called the "Beckham Boot." This for all the world is like a boot one would wear if one was going skiing but is comfortable enough for walking with the aid of crutches. It is called the "Beckham Boot" because David Beckham the footballer was at one time fitted with this type boot after a serious injury to his foot. A few days more in the hospital getting used to this boot and the crutches, I'm sent home to convalesce. The people in the hospital tell me it should take about another six weeks before I can discard this boot.

Tomorrow is the start of the fourteenth week since my accident and only three days ago have I discarded the boot. But, I'm still on crutches. Today is the first day that I can really say I'm on the mend as both the back and the foot are feeling fairly good, and so unlike Johnny Curran there is Thank God a flicker of light at the end of my tunnel.

A Norry, Never.

Not from this parish,
Sure I don't think that makes much odds.
No racism up here,
For a blowin from the Southside.
Domiciled among strangers,
These last fifty years.
But, with a wife from the Northside,
I've managed to survive.
Sometimes the sly remark,
"To find love, you had to cross the bridge boy."
She was a Sunbeam girl,
And I didn't even know where the Sunbeam was.
One of my friends said,
"It's somewhere out near Blackpool."
"That's a long way from here" I said.
"You have a bike, haven't you?"
"Yeh, I wonder what they make out there?
"Nylons and Knickers" He said.
"Go 'way ou' that you're having me on?"
"That's what I heard anyway."
Last night I said I'd meet her after work.
"By the Spangle Hill gate." She said
"I'll finish at six." She said.
Spangle Hill? I've heard the name somewhere.
I hope I'll find the place,
Maybe I'll give her a crossbar home.
And now eight kids and thirteen grandchildren later,
I'm torn between three loves.
My wife, my family,
And the place where I was born.
And, though my feet are here in Churchfield,
My heart is in Quaker Road.